D1362919

Caroline Green is an experienced freelance journalist who has written stories since she was a little girl. She vividly remembers a family walk when she was ten years old when she was so preoccupied with thoughts of her new 'series' that she almost walked into a tree.

Caroline lives in North London with her husband, two sporty sons and one very bouncy labrador retriever.

Her first novel, *Dark Ride*, was longlisted for the Branford Boase award and won the RoNA Young Adult award. *Cracks* and *Hold Your Breath* have both also received high critical acclaim and fan praise.

FRAGMENTS

CAROLINE GREEN

Piccadilly

Pete, Joe and Harry.
This one's for you.

First published in Great Britain in 2014
by Piccadilly Press,
A Templar/Bonnier publishing company
Deepdene Lodge, Deepdene Avenue,
Dorking, Surrey, RH5 4AT
www.piccadillypress.co.uk

Text copyright © Caroline Green, 2014

A catalogue record for this book is available
from the British Library

ISBN: 978 1 84812 364 9 (paperback)

Also available as an ebook

1 3 5 7 9 10 8 6 4 2

Printed and bound by CPI Group (UK) Ltd, Croydon, CR0 4YY

PART I

YORKSHIRE

CHAPTER 1

puppet

Everyone says, 'It's so quiet here.'

Like that's a good thing.

But it just makes the noise inside my head louder.

I'm sitting halfway up the hill, under the shade of some big old tree, thinking and trying not to. I wish I could switch my brain off. Or forget for even a minute.

Forget that I've lost my best friend. My brother. I guess you could say he was my whole family.

When they told me that Jax was dead it was too . . . *huge* to be true. Their mouths were flapping away and this white noise was coming out. How could he be gone? I didn't believe it. Even now I keep expecting the daft lummox to walk into the room and make one of his crap jokes.

But deep inside, in a raw, dark place, I know that he's gone. For good.

I bury my face in my arms. The rough bark of the tree scratches me through my top and I press myself a little harder against it. I want it to *hurt*, to distract me from crying again.

'Hey.'

I didn't hear anyone coming.

My head snaps up and I squint into the brightness. All I can make out is a shape haloed by sunlight. My spirits lift the tiniest bit.

Cal sits down next to me and stretches out his long legs.

We kissed earlier. It was nice. Really nice. But now I'm shy again. He clears his throat. Maybe he is too.

'So how is it?' I say. I try really hard to sound interested, the way I should be.

He hesitates and I sneak a glance. His eyes are full of happy wonder, as though he's seeing something too awesome to describe. His cheek kinks, like he's holding a smile inside.

'It's . . . amazing,' he says. Then, drily, 'And *really* bloody weird.'

'I bet.'

Weird probably doesn't even begin to cover it.

About two hours ago, Cal met his parents for the first time in, like, twelve years or something.

He was taken from them as a baby and kept in a

government research laboratory called the Facility. They experimented on him and put a chip in his brain. They also did something with brain tissue from a dead boy that meant some of his memories belonged to someone else. I'm fuzzy on the details. It makes me go a bit funny to think about it.

We've been staying with resistance people from the rebel group Torch, who want to bring our government, the Securitat, down. They call them 'terrorists' on the news but I know the truth. Torch are the good guys in this cruel, messed-up world we live in. They rescued Cal from that place and tried to rescue Jax too, but, well, he wasn't so lucky.

I glance at the boy next to me. He's gazing into the distance. I like that we can be still together; it's good to know he's there, even if I don't feel like talking.

But guilt twists inside me when I think about how I've kept out of the way today. I didn't want to see the big, happy reunion scene he had with his mum and dad. Don't need to be reminded that he now has people to love him and give him a home.

Yeah, I know how that sounds.

What kind of nasty person could resent Cal getting lucky? After everything he went through?

A person like me, that's who. And don't think I don't hate myself for it.

Cal makes another throat-clearing noise.

'So,' he says, all casual, 'they, um, want to meet you. Do you feel up to it?'

5

A feeling of total, overwhelming tiredness presses in on me. I wish I could make myself into the tiniest thing that would blow away on the wind, like dandelion fluff.

I picture the scene. Me going down there with a polite, friendly face. They'll be all, 'It's so good to meet you, Kyla,' and 'Cal has told us all about you, Kyla.' And then they'll go away with him, ready to start their life together. Cal will leave me, just like everyone else has.

God, I really am the worst.

So I force the sides of my mouth up and say, 'Yeah, course! You go on ahead and I'll come down in a little while . . .'

Cal looks at me and reaches over to take my hand in his warm, dry one. Then he leans over and gently presses his lips to mine. 'Thank you,' he murmurs and I feel the words as soft breath on my face. For a tiny second, the kiss ignites a weak flame inside me, like I can imagine being happy again, with him. Then it snuffs out. He'll be gone soon, won't he?

'Wait,' I say and fumble for my phone. He makes a quizzical face as I snap a photo. I shrug, feeling silly now.

'Help us remember a special day,' I mumble and force a grin. He grins back before walking down the hill. His hurry to get back shows in every long stride.

Letting the smile drop from my face is a relief, like putting down a heavy bag.

My vision blurs and wobbles and I know I can't stop the tears. All I've done is cry for days but somehow my stupid eyes keep on leaking.

I snuffle and sob for a bit until my chest starts to squeeze and cramp. Fumbling in my trouser pockets again, my fingers close around the breather stick. One of the Torch people at the farmhouse, Sam, is a doctor. She gave it to me for my asthma. I've never had anything that good before. I put the small Y-shaped pen to my nose and breathe the sweet drug into my lungs, which instantly start to relax.

I try to get myself together. I promised Cal I'd go meet the parents and I have to do it. But I can't go looking like this . . .

I rub under my eyes and try to pat my hair down a bit.

There's a bee somewhere nearby, buzzing away, and I look around. I don't want to get stung. Those things get infected and you're in trouble. It might even be one of those super-resistant malaria mozzies I've heard about. I squint into the bright sunlight, trying to see where the sound's coming from. My heartbeat seems too loud in my own ears too.

A cloud passes over my head.

And then icy shock fills my bones.

It's not a mosquito or a bee or a heartbeat I'm hearing . . .

Three helicopters fly in formation above, black and spiky with weapons, blades thumping a rhythm that vibrates in my chest and head. Buzz drones – evil, bug-like CCTV cameras – swarm around them, darting and dodging but flying in some sort of order. Recording every moment of the flight.

Why are they here? Maybe they're on their way somewhere else? There's nothing out here except farms and sheep. I expect them to turn west towards Lancaster.

Please turn . . .

But they continue in a straight line. The engine sounds dip to a throaty rumble that turns my stomach over with dread.

They're heading for the farmhouse, the house that everyone said was so safe. Everyone is in there. Julia, Sam and Mo from Torch. Cal. Cal's mum and dad . . .

I'm on my feet, screaming pointless warnings, but I can't seem to move. I can't run down the hill to warn them. I know I'll die if I do.

All I can do is watch helplessly as the first missile explodes into the roof of the farmhouse. The other two helicopters peel away and blast the outbuildings of the farm. A plume of black and red spouts through the roof and then the whole farm goes up. Shockwaves slam into me and I fall, my face hitting the mud. I feel my cheek rip and taste blood and dirt.

I don't know how long I'm there, face down in the mud. I drift in and out of the world. After a while, things come into bright, painful focus again. Groaning, I sit up slowly. The side of my face hurts and when I put my fingers there, they come away smeared with blood and mud. Then, with what feels like a superhuman effort, I force myself to turn over and look at the farmhouse.

Except there is no farmhouse now. There's only a

blackened, smoking skeleton of a building. Time hangs around me as though the world has stopped. The air is bitter and smoky, hot and toxic. All I can hear are snapping sounds as flames eat the remains of the building. My throat burns and I bend double, coughing and wheezing.

Everything hurts but it all feels like it's on the surface. I can't seem to take in what has happened. I'm sort of numb. Everyone I've come to know in these past couple of weeks has been killed in one fell swoop. No one could have survived that blast. Why can't I feel anything? I should check inside. But I won't. I haven't got the courage to go down there and risk seeing burned bodies. Seeing Cal . . .

Cal.

OH GOD . . .

Reality slams into me then and I'm on my hands and knees, heaving bitterness onto the grass, my stomach cramping and aching with every spasm that passes through me.

I hear someone crying in a weird way, like a mewling cat, and then I realise it's me. I wish I could make my legs work but all my limbs are like jelly. I feel like one of those puppet things people used to have in old times. I wish someone else would make my strings work because I need to move. I don't know where to, but I can't go near the house. I've heard they booby trap the remains of places they've destroyed, to stop looters. But that's not why I don't go. I can't bear to see the bodies inside.

They're all I had left. And they're all gone.

I don't know what to do.

I don't know where to go.

All I know is that I'm in danger here. I don't want to die too. I don't want to be like those bodies. I have to get away.

Somewhere.

Anywhere.

CHAPTER 2

monster

Some time later, I don't know how long, I'm standing at the side of a road. I don't remember getting here. I think I just walked until I ran out of grass. My ears are funny from the blast. Maybe I'm deaf. I don't care. My face hurts and I wish I could stop this *shaking*.

I think about trying to get a lift but the first car that approaches me slows down and then speeds up again. I see the round, frightened eyes of a woman and a young boy as they accelerate away and I realise I must look bad. When you see someone covered in blood and bruises these days, you look the other way. You don't offer lifts, even if it's just a girl like me. No one wants to bring trouble to their door.

I need to get out of sight. If I could just find somewhere to lie down so I can think properly.

I cross the road and keep walking towards more fields. There are cows in one and high fences all round so I have to go a long way around, through scratchy grass-like stuff that itches and covers me in tiny pods. I don't know what it is. I hate the countryside.

This makes me laugh. Me, of all people, being stranded in the countryside! I'm laughing really hard, so hard that my sides actually hurt and I'm gasping for breath and then it's not funny and I'm scaring myself a bit.

When I was little and stropping about something Mum would poke me in the side and tickle me until I laughed and forgot why I was upset. *Give me a smile, Kylaboo*, she would say. Oh no. Big mistake to think about Mum. Mum is dead too. Everybody is dead . . .

Just keep walking.

Keep walking.

Don't think.

Eventually I can see buildings ahead. I think it's a farm because of the big barns in grey metal. But as I said, I'm not big on country things. There's a fence along the back here. A large, red-brick house stands just beyond this area.

The fence is high, covered in spiked coils of barbed wire. Bound to be CCTV-ed up too. No way I can get in there. But still I walk towards the buildings. If I can only curl up somewhere for a while and rest, maybe clean up my face. I can't think at the moment. I need to lie down for a bit. If only I could lie down . . .

When I get close to the fence I see that there is a tree just outside, branches spreading over towards the curly, vicious wire. Hope flares in me like a struck match. If there's one thing I can do, it's climb. It was the only reason Zander let me stay. He was the crime lord me and Jax lived with when Cal came into our lives. I was good for shimmying up buildings and getting through difficult spaces to get to his pickings.

There are engine-y rumbles from inside the grey barns and shouts from men working in there. I do a quick check for cameras. There's one on the fence that moves slowly from side to side like an unblinking eye. I crouch low and wait for it to turn the other way. Then I run, gasping and wincing at the pains in my body – face, side, hands – all the way to the tree. Heart hammering, I hide behind it and begin to climb up, using the lower branches and knobbly places as footholds. I slip a little, though, and the inside of my arm scrapes down the bark. I have to bite my lip to stop myself from crying out.

Soon I'm inside the rich, glossy leaves at the heart of the tree. All the rain has made everything bright green. That's what someone once would have said, anyway. It hurts my eyes. There's no place for beauty now.

I've got a good view of the yard, though. A large lorry is open at the back and a couple of small, pick-up type vehicles are moving pallets around. Men in overalls are shouting things out to each other. There's only, what, five of them? I'm sure I can slip past them.

I don't have a plan once I get in. I just want to lie down.

I crawl along a sturdy branch of the tree, inching my sore body forward. The leaves camouflage my dirty, tattered clothes. Soon I'm over the barbed wire. I've done this so many times I know not to look at the metal teeth that could chew my skin open. I twist and jump, thumping to the ground. I land on my feet, though, like a cat. Maybe I have nine lives. Maybe I'm on my ninth.

I'm in-between two of the barns. I sidle up to the wall towards the front to peek out.

One of the pick-ups is whirring away down to the left, taking boxes from the lorry. A tall, fat man is talking into a headset and gesturing to the guy driving. I look left and right. Across the way there's a lower building with horses poking long snouts out of windows. Stables. That'll do.

I run across the dirt, out in the open. All my nerve endings seem to shriek at the certainty of being caught. The door is open and I hurl myself inside. Horses shift and toss their heads back, checking me out. Quickly scanning the stables I see one stall at the end that seems to be free and run to it, throwing myself inside and pulling the door closed.

It stinks of horse poo in here and I wrinkle my nose. Pain flares in my cheek again and tears prick my eyes. But for the moment, I think I'm safe.

Live moment by moment. That's the only way. I learned that when Mum died of the pig-flu epidemic that killed off about a quarter of the country.

I stayed in our flat for a few weeks until they started clearing them out. Said they had to beat the infection there. I didn't know what was going to happen to me. I had nowhere to live. I'd heard what happened to kids in care. Either you got recruited into the army, or . . . well, I heard worse stuff too, about ending up as slaves one way or another.

I sort of gave up for a day or two. And then I bumped into Jax, who used to live on the same floor. Hadn't paid much attention to him before, I guess. He'd lived with a foster mum who ended up being carted off for terrorist offences. He looked as lost as I felt. So we sort of hooked up. Learned to live on the streets, stealing to stay alive. That was before we met Zander and he took us on.

Anyway, the point is that I have lost everything before and I found a way to live. If I can force myself to think only about *the very next thing I need*, and not look at the big, scary picture, I can stop myself from going completely crazy. I've been through bad times before and I somehow survived. Can I get through this? I don't know yet. All I can do is clean my face and try to rest for a bit.

There's a sort of open metal box on the wall and when I look into it, I can see a thin puddle of greenish water. No good. But horses need fresh water, don't they? So there must be some in one of the other stalls.

The thought of going into an enclosed space with one of those hot, snorting monsters fills me with dread. I'll get kicked to death. And do they bite? I don't know, do I?

But I'm suddenly so thirsty I think I'll die without some water to drink, let alone to clean my face up with. Decisively, I push open the door again and listen. I can hear a beep-beep-beep outside. I reckon it's the lorry reversing out of the yard. I slip into the next stall where a massive, conker-brown horse eyes me with a starey, mad expression.

Horses are weird. Its eyes are messing with my head a bit. Like it can see inside. *Don't be stupid, Kyla* . . .

'Hey, horse,' I say, dumbly. My voice is all croaky and doesn't sound like me at all. My cheek hurts when I talk. 'Good boy. Nice horsey. Gonna share a drink with me, yeah? Good horsey.'

The stall stinks of hot animal sweat and worse. For a second I'm overwhelmed by the size of this muscle machine. It seems to fill the space. The metal water container is on the side in this stall, rather than at the front. It's right by the bloody horse. I gently edge forwards. The horse makes a snorty-snuffly noise and its nostrils flare in a scary way. Its head is up and it shifts its big heavy feet. Maybe this is what horses do right before they charge at you . . .

'Nice horsey, nice horsey, just share a little drinkie with old Kyla, OK?' I'm mumbling all sorts of rubbish as I edge towards the water box. The horse snuffles again and steps back, away from me. Maybe it's scared of *me*? This gives me confidence for half a second until I realise what it would be like if this enormous, snorting monster panicked in such a small space. I picture myself trampled to death and my heart rate kicks up a few notches.

But I force myself to take another couple of steps before reaching a shaky hand into the metal box. There is water in there but it's warm and yucky. There's probably horse spit in it and the thought makes me gag. But I'm so thirsty I reach over anyway and splash some onto my face, never letting my eyes stray from the horse's. We're eyeballing each other now. The water doesn't smell or anything and I ignore the bits of straw in there, cupping my hands to slosh the warm wetness in the general direction of my mouth. It only makes me more thirsty and before I know what I'm doing, I've dipped my whole face in to drink, like I'm a horse too.

My face screams with pain. Maybe I'm really badly hurt. Oh God, what if the wound gets infected? Antibiotics are more precious than gold these days. The ones Cal gave me for my chest before have all gone now. I *have* to get my cheek clean. I plunge my face into the box and frantically rub until the water swirls pink.

After a bit I stop and edge slowly backwards from the stall. The horse dips its head and, for a crazy second, I think it's saying goodbye. This makes me want to cry and I have to bite down on my hand to stop myself.

I slip back out of the door and into the next stall. I bunch the straw up as high as it will go just inside the door, hoping that anyone giving a brief glance over won't see me unless they look carefully. Trembling all over, I drop down and cover myself.

It's like being jabbed with a thousand needles and all the

scratches I hadn't noticed before on my arms suddenly hurt like hell. I thought it would be sweet-smelling, soft and comfortable. Let me tell you, straw is nothing like that. Must have got the romantic view from those stories Mum used to read from her Bible, the one her own mum brought from Jamaica all those years ago.

I'm so tired that, even with the itching and the horse pooey smells and the pain in my face, I think I can sleep. I close my eyes and try to make myself small, drawing my knees up like I'm a baby again. The images rattle through my head straight away: the helicopters with the beating blades, the explosion, the feeling of the hard dirt against my face. They play over and over and I can't stop them coming.

'*I'm so sorry*,' I whisper through my dry, sore lips. Maybe I made it happen. I was jealous and now everyone's dead. This feels like poison inside me. I can never un-know it . . . I can never undo it . . .

Helicopter blades thump and then turn into wings flapping with a heartbeat rhythm. Black bird-like things closing in on me with their claws outstretched, with tattered, smoking wings.

But someone is here to help me now. A good angel. Blond, wavy hair curls around a small face with a pointy chin. Sparkly blue eyes with long sandy lashes. Freckles smattered across a cute, snub nose. A small pink tongue runs across pale, dry lips.

The face is right over mine.

Then I understand that I'm not dreaming. This is real.

CHAPTER 3

picnic

I scoot backwards like a crab, straw flying up around me so I start sneezing.

'Bless you!' she says with a tinkly laugh, except it comes out as 'Bleth' and I notice the gap where she has lost her front milk teeth.

'Who are you?' I whisper. I'm looking beyond her, expecting to see a couple of Counterinsurgency and Anti-Terrorism Squad dudes all tooled up there, ready to cart me off. I feel around in the straw with one hand, not moving my eyes from hers. Maybe I can find a stone or something to throw at them when they come for me.

'I'm Ariella. I'm six. Who are you? And why are you in my daddy's barn?'

She's stopped smiling. I realise I might be scaring her now.

'Um, I'm . . .' Shall I tell her my name? 'I'm Kyla.' Too late. I'm not properly thinking straight. I have a ferocious headache over one eye and my cheek . . . *man*, that hurts. I lift my hand slowly to it and dab with my fingers. There's a big semi-circle of skin missing, I think. Pain zigzags over my cheek and up to my scalp.

'What did you do to your face?' she says curiously.

I hesitate.

'I fell.' I know it's lame. I expect her eyes to narrow in suspicion. I'm still thinking whoever is with her is about to come storming in here too. 'I hurt it on the ground.' But the corners of her mouth turn down and her eyes seem to shine a little more.

'It looks really sore,' she says sadly.

'Yes, it really is sore,' I agree. I find that I'm nodding weirdly. I never know what to say to children. Jax was great at that. Sometimes he had half the kids on the estate hanging off him like Christmas lights on a tree.

Ariella's face brightens. 'My mummy has special cream that she put on her tummy when Kit came out of it. He's my brother and he's boring because he cries a lot.' She makes a disgusted face that's almost funny. 'Mummy says the special cream made her tummy better really quickly. Shall I bring it for you?'

I sit up a bit straighter and attempt a smile. Which hurts my face.

'That would be great. Do you think you could bring me

water and something to eat too, um, Ariella?'

There's a beat while she considers me and then she smiles again. 'We've got flapjacks. Do you like flapjacks? I do but I don't like cheese. So I won't bring any.'

I keep smiling, even though it hurts my face.

'Got it, no cheese then.' I try to sound bright. 'Anything else is fine. Thank you. And, um, Ariella?'

She has turned away but she looks back at me, blowing a spiral of blond hair away from her face. 'Hmm?'

'Can it just be our secret? Me being in here? I might get into trouble with your mummy and daddy and then I'd have to go away. So can we make it a special secret?' I feel like I'm pleading with her.

A sly look crosses her face then and she lifts her finger to her lips, miming '*Shhh.*' I do it back and she leaves the barn.

It takes her almost an hour to come back, according to my phone, which is somehow still working. I'm thinking about getting the hell out of here when I hear footsteps outside the stall. The door creaks open.

I didn't really notice what she was wearing before. But I think she must have changed. Now she has on a fancy-dress witch costume in shiny green material. It's all twisted around her waist. I think the buttoning has gone a bit wrong along the line. She has a streak of something purple around her lips (my money's on Ribena) and her bare legs are thrust into pink-spotted wellies that have mud thickly crusted around the soles.

She's carrying a large backpack decorated in pictures of Gomez, the annoying rat thing off the telly that kids go mad for. With another sly look back at me she kicks the stall door closed with a neat back heel before wrenching open the bag and tipping out the contents, which are:

– A packet of baby wipes.

– A bottle of cherryade.

– Several squashed flapjacks spilling out of a pink paper napkin.

– Two boxes of raisins.

– One of those ultra-thin sleeping bags that crumple into nothing. (Zander had one and they cost a bomb.) They're *brilliant* ...

– A pot of something cosmetic. 'Mummy's cream', no doubt.

– A hairbrush and several butterfly hair-clips.

– A small plastic Gomez figure.

– A lipstick without a lid ...

OK ...

Ariella frowns anxiously at me. 'Did I do well?' she says.

'You did brilliantly,' I say, croaky because my throat is dry. 'You're a total star.'

Her face lights up with pleasure and she unselfconsciously lifts up her skirt over chubby knees so she can sit down cross-legged.

It's quickly obvious that she intends to have some of this stuff too. To her, it's just a picnic. When she cracks open the

22

bottle of cherryade and takes a lusty drink before me, it's all I can do not to snatch it away from the greedy brat before she can glug the lot. I clear my throat and she makes startled eyes and blushes.

'O-oh,' she says, hiccupping. 'I should let you have some first. You're probably much more thirstier than I am. Mummy says I'm selfish and need to stop putting myself before everyone else.' Her little mouth has gone all turned down again. I can't help thinking she's cute now, despite the not-being-keen-on-kids thing.

'I don't think you're selfish. I think you're a very kind person,' I say and lift the bottle to my lips. It's so sweet and good as it runs into my mouth that I gulp too fast and a wave of nausea comes up inside. I get a weird urge to cry because I'm so grateful. Ariella's smiling shyly now as she goes up onto her knees and neatly picks up a squashed bit of flapjack between finger and thumb to offer to me.

I bob my head and say, 'Why thank you, milady.'

Ariella giggles throatily and stuffs a huge piece of flapjack into her mouth sideways.

I eat quickly and then grab a box of raisins before she can nick it. I wasn't hungry until I started eating but now I'm ravenous. I give little reassuring smiles to Ariella as I scoff and she grins back. She seems to have got the message and hasn't taken the other box of raisins.

'So why are you in my daddy's barn?' she says suddenly. My insides plummet. I was hoping she'd forgotten about that. But she's not stupid. She knows that finding a girl covered in bruises in her dad's barn isn't exactly normal, even these days.

'Well,' I say slowly, searching in my brain for the right words to use. 'My house burned down.' God, why did I say that? I'm trying to think how to put it so she won't get scared and grass me up. 'Er . . . and I have nowhere to go now. I've lost all my things.'

Her eyes are practically circles now and her bottom lip hangs open, still glistening with cherryade.

'Did your mummy and daddy get hurt?' she says.

'I haven't got a mummy or a daddy,' I say carefully. 'But my friends got hurt.'

Ariella's eyes fill with fat tears. 'You must be *very* sad,' she says fiercely.

'Yes.' I'm doing that mad nodding thing again. 'I am. But, er, I might get into trouble if anyone knows I'm here so I need you to still keep this as your best secret, OK?'

Weirdly, she doesn't question the bit about getting into trouble. I don't know why. Maybe it's the world we live in. Even kids know it's best just to shut up sometimes. They know that people, teachers even, are there some days and then gone the next. And it's wise not to ask what happened to them.

Ariella goes to take the raisins and then draws her hand back again, looking at me through lowered lids. I don't know what to say. I have an image of her suddenly yelling for her parents. I need to keep her sweet. Maybe she can get me some clothes and once I'm cleaned up I can get on my way.

'Your hair's all tangly,' she says. 'Shall I make it nice for you?'

I smile. 'That would be lovely. But can I clean up my sore face first?'

Ten minutes later, I'm gritting my teeth as she claws the brush through my tangled hair. I've used the baby wipes to clean up my cheek and slathered on some of her mum's cream. It smells horrible but as soon as it's on my face, the pain eases up. I endure a few more minutes of her tugging and try to explain that my hair is different from hers because I'm mixed race, and then she's shoving in the various butterfly clips all around my face.

She sits back and surveys her work, giving a deep sigh. 'You're pretty,' she says. 'Even with a sore, poorly face.'

I smile at her. 'So are you,' I say. 'Even with cherryade all round your chops.'

Her belly laugh at this is infectious. I don't know what *I've* got to laugh about, though. I still have nowhere to go and everyone is . . . everyone is dead.

I feel myself freefalling inside and for a second I'm scared I'm going to start howling at the pain threatening to engulf me. Ariella puts a chubby hand on mine. I look down and notice that a couple of my nails still have faint traces of the purple sparkly polish I put on a lifetime ago. Glancing up I see that Ariella has her finger to her lips.

And that's when I realise someone is calling her. A woman, sounding irritable.

'Where are you? Ari-e-llaaaaa!'

She leans over and whispers in my ear, her breath hot and fierce. 'I'll come back in the morning. I'll bring some of Mummy's clothes and some breakfast.'

I nod gratefully and she opens the door of the stall with surprising care. I hear the shushy sound of her wellies in the straw as she leaves the stables.

'There you are! What have you got all over your face?' says the woman, who I presume to be her mother. 'It's bath-time! I've been calling for ages.'

'Sorry, Mummy,' Ariella replies in a sing-song way and I hear the voices recede.

The light is fading now and when I look at my watch I see it's after eight in the evening. I still don't know whether I should try to get away but I have nowhere to go. I can't seem to think straight. Maybe a night here will help sort out my head a bit?

And I am really tired. Cold now, too.

Plus, and this is the worst bit . . . I need to pee. I go into the stall next door, where the big old horse now stands with its head drooping and eyes closed and pee in the corner of the stall.

'Sorry, horse,' I say under my breath. I wash my hands in the water box and feel guilty about that too.

Back in the empty stall and feeling relieved, I open the

feather-light sleeping bag and wriggle inside it. I pull the hood part over my head and try to bunch some straw underneath to make a pillow. Then I close my eyes.

My dreams aren't of death and violence this time.

They're much crueller.

I dream about Mum, stirring something at the cooker, her big hips swaying as she hums along to a song on the radio. She turns and gives me a look of love that's like being wrapped in layers of silk. Then I'm sitting with Jax on the sofa at Zander's place. We're playing a game of Insurgent Cell on the X Station and although I'm not really fussed about video games, I'm beating his ass as usual. I tease him and he laughs, because he's like that, Jax. Never bears a grudge. His face changes into Cal's and he's leaning over me for a kiss. Our lips touch and it's all sweet. Then he draws back and his nice brown eyes crinkle in a smile.

Happiness feels like warm honey seeping up my spine. I've got everyone I need. My family. My best bud. My boy. That's when my eyes crack open, sore and swollen, and it all rushes at me like a car going ninety. There's only me now. And BAM there it is again, the pain. I curl up in a ball, wrapping my arms around myself. It feels worse than ever before, so bad I think it might kill me this time. I wish it would.

I never knew that sadness was a physical thing before. I've learned a lot about it lately. I could get myself a PhD in heartache. My body rocks as waves of grief slam into me but no more tears come. Crying is too easy. Getting up on your feet and *living* is the hard thing. But what choice do I have?

I have to find a way to carry on. Somehow. And that's when I start to think I've been getting it all wrong until now. I wanted people around me; friends, maybe a boyfriend too. But everyone I care about gets snatched away from me. It's love that brings all this pain. I need to learn not to care about anyone. My insides feel as though they are raw and bleeding with all the losses. I have to make myself hard inside. I thought I was so tough but I'm not, not really. There's only me now.

I need to find a way to carry on and live.

Some time later I hear light footsteps outside the stall and the door creaks open again. Ariella's small white face pokes around the door and a smile lights it up.

'I thought I'd dreamed you up!' she says, coming in. 'Or that if you were real, you'd have gone away by now.'

'Still here,' I say lamely. My eyes sting from the crying and my body aches from sleeping in the damn straw. I feel hollow inside. Scooped out.

Ariella's outfit is a bit less out-there today. She's dressed in cut-off jeans and a silvery T-shirt. Her hair is all matted at the back. She has the Gomez bag with her and starts taking out what looks like a couple of bagels, wrapped in cellophane, and two cartons of orange juice. My mouth instantly waters and, yet again, my body reminds me it needs some fuel. I pick up a carton of orange juice first and pretty much down it in one go.

'Mummy is very sad today,' she says matter of factly as

28

she hands me one of the bagels, like we'd just been talking about this.

'Oh?' I say and unwrap the bagel. The smell of peanut butter hits the back of my throat. I've always hated it. 'Um, are they both peanut butter?'

She doesn't blink as she swaps bagels with me. I open this one and see jam inside. Phew. I take a huge bite and feel the energy instantly start to come back.

'Daddy gets cross when she cries and says she has to pull herself together,' continues Ariella.

'Oh dear.' I don't know what to say.

But this doesn't seem to bother Ariella much. 'Mummy says if she had some *more help around the place she'd be able to get on top of things*. But then they fight. I don't like it when they shout.' I almost laugh at the grown-up voice she puts on for a minute.

Her eyes are lowered as she munches on the bagel and we eat in silence for a little while. Then she does that sly thing with her eyes again.

'I didn't tell anyone about you,' she says and something makes fear tingle up the back of my neck.

I put down the almost finished bagel and look at her but she won't meet my gaze.

She's told someone. I know it.

'If you have mentioned me, even by accident, I need to know,' I say, trying to keep my voice light, although anger and fear rise inside me.

Her cheeks flood with colour as she finally meets my gaze.

'I didn't tell Mummy about you!' she says. 'I just said I had a secret and that I wouldn't share it, that's all. I'm cross with Mummy because she never plays with me any more. What are you doing?'

I've jumped to my feet and am frantically rolling up the sleeping bag. Got to get away from here. Her mum sounds like she has her own worries but I don't think I can stay here. It was mad to think I could, even for a day or so. I just needed to get myself together but maybe I'm as together as I'm ever going to be.

'Where are you going?' Ariella's tone is panicky and too loud. I shush her, trying to sound gentle in case she has a full-on tantrum and starts wailing.

'I need to go.'

'But you can't!'

I don't hear anyone coming but a face is suddenly there, above the top of the door of the stall.

CHAPTER 4

a very experienced babysitter

I t's a woman in, I don't know, her thirties, maybe. She has dark hair that's pulled into a ponytail. The roots are greasy. Her eyes are puffy and her face pale. She gasps and lifts a hand to her mouth before pushing the door open violently.

That's when I see the blob shape of a baby, strapped to her chest in one of those sling things. All I can see is a tuft of gingery hair poking out the top, two scrawny little legs with the feet covered and a hand with a tiny, wrinkled, bunched fist.

'Who the bloody hell are *you*?' says the woman. Ariella scrambles to her feet.

'Mummy, this is Kyla and she's my friend!'

'Mummy' fixes me with a look that makes my scalp shrivel.

'I repeat,' she says icily, 'who ARE you? And why are you in our stables?'

I swallow. My mouth has gone completely dry. I wonder if I should push her out of the way and run but I can't bring myself to do it when she's carrying that baby.

'I'm sorry,' I mumble. 'I've got nowhere to go.' Words start tumbling out of my mouth. 'I was in care in, um . . .' – I frantically search in my brain for the name of the nearest town – 'Arnley . . . and the place got closed down. They wanted to ship us to London and I didn't want to go so I ran away. I'm really sorry. I'll go . . .' I don't know where all that rubbish just came from. I wouldn't believe me if I was her.

'Yes, I think you'd better be off,' she says sharply.

'*Nooo!*' Ariella whines. 'Mumm*eee*! I want her to stay!'

Her mother opens and closes her mouth, colour rising in her face. For a moment the resemblance between her and Ariella is strong. That's when a thin, high cry comes from the woman's chest and the baby's legs do a sort of frog kick.

'Oh hell!' says the woman. 'You've set Kit off now!' She places her hand at the back of its head and starts jiggling, which just makes the baby's wails take on a juddering, shaky sound.

Ariella is properly crying now. 'Please, Mummy!' she says. '*Please* don't make her go!'

I look uncertainly between them, still not sure whether I should bolt.

'Look, you'd better come into the house for a while,'

says the woman with a sigh. 'I can't think straight when he's crying like this.'

I let out a slow breath. Maybe she can see I'm not dangerous.

Ariella manages to give me a tear-stained smile while her mother's eyes are focused downwards on the baby. She turns and gives a gesture for us to follow.

We follow her out of the barn. The sky is a flat grey today but, even so, the light hurts my eyes after the dimness of the stable. A headache spasms across my forehead and for the first time since I woke up, my cheek throbs. I'm thirsty, dirty and sore and I need the toilet. I haven't got the energy to run. Something Mum used to say comes into my mind: 'What will be, will be.'

There isn't anyone else in the farmyard, which seems weird after all the activity here yesterday. Maybe it's a Sunday or something. Do farmers work on Sundays? I can't even remember a time when days of the week meant anything, anyway. Working for Zander wasn't exactly a Monday-to-Saturday job.

We pass several of the big warehouse barns and come to a huge gate over a cattle-grid. Ariella's mother swings the gate open and waits for us to come through, avoiding my eye all the time. That's when I know there's no point entertaining any ideas about her letting me stay here and play at farmers. She's getting straight on the phone to the police after she's calmed that shrieking baby down.

I could run, but the thing is, I *really* need the toilet. There's no way I'm going in any straw again. I've still got scratches on my bum from last night. I reckon I've got fifteen minutes, tops, before she's calling the cops. I'll go to the loo. Might get a drink of water and see if there's any money lying around too.

We cross a narrow road. Mrs Miserable opens another gate. There's a sign saying *Craydale Farm*. The house I could see from up the hill is up a short driveway. It's old-fashioned looking and red brick with rows of windows criss-crossed with metal. Completely different from the modern one that I stayed in with Cal and everyone. The one that got blown to bits.

No, no, don't think about that now, I tell myself. Got enough on my plate.

We crunch up the gravel driveway, the baby-siren wailing the entire time. Ariella keeps her mouth shut but shoots glances at me every few seconds.

Parked in front of the house is one of those big hybrid SUVs. The chassis is so high up most people need to use the elevating platform to get into the thing, or so Jax told me, who loved these cars.

A huge grey dog springs up outside the front door. I stop abruptly. I don't do dogs. And this is no handbag mutt. This thing is more like a horse. It's the colour of a rainy sky and has eyes that seem to look right through to my juicy innards. It goes to nudge its massive head against me and my hands fly up in self-defence.

The dog comes up to Ariella's shoulder but she casually elbows it out of the way.

'Lie down, Brutus!' she says crossly. To my amazement, the beast trots away and slumps down with a weary sigh.

The front door opens and Ariella's mother walks right in, glancing back over her shoulder as if to check I'm still there.

'Can I use the toilet?' I say quickly. She stops, looking at me with a blank expression.

'One through there,' she says. 'Ariella, you go with her.'

Yeah, because I'm gonna nick your soap, you stuck-up cow, I think, even though I might.

Ariella leads me to a downstairs toilet where the walls are painted bright blue and covered in small pictures of flowers in matching frames.

When I come out, Ariella is waiting for me. She smiles a bit weakly. I reckon even *she's* lost hope of me and her mother bonding.

'Mummy's feeding Kit in the kitchen,' she says in a conspiratorial way. I nod and follow her through to a big room, brightly lit by spotlights in the ceiling. There's a huge kitchen table and swanky metal countertops everywhere. Mum would have done anything for a kitchen like this. It's a bit of a mess, though. There are dirty dishes piled up next to the sink and the table is covered with baby stuff: a changing mat, nappies and one of those colourful gym things babies lie under doing God knows what.

I stand in the doorway, shuffling my feet. I don't really know what to do. But I'd like a drink before I go. I'm sort of curious too. I'm not getting vibes that the police have been called yet.

Ariella's mother is sitting at the table. The baby's head is turned towards a huge white breast covered in horrible blue veins. The boob is bigger than the baby's head. I decide there and then that I am never, *ever* having kids. I snap my gaze elsewhere.

'Come in for a minute,' she says, her eyes hard, as though she knows exactly what I was thinking.

I look at Ariella, who nods vigorously from over by the fridge, where she is getting out a large bottle of Coke. She busies herself slopping it into three plastic cups.

I slide onto a chair and regard her mother warily.

'Are you going to call the police?' I didn't know I was planning to say this until the words came out. I'd rather know where I stand, is all.

'Should I?' she fires back at me, her eyes never leaving my face. The baby is making a sort of grunty slurping sound and it's sort of fascinating in a creepy way.

'I haven't broken any laws or done anything wrong,' I say, adding *for a good two weeks* silently in my head. Ariella puts a cup each down in front of me and her mother, spilling some on the table as she does so. But her mother doesn't seem to care and raises hers to her lips. Ariella sits down at the table and noisily glugs her own drink.

'What happened to your face?' says her mother.

'I tripped over,' I shoot back, self-consciously lifting

my hand to my throbbing cheek.

There's a silence for a moment, broken only by the baby's weird slurping.

'Can she stay with us, Mummy?' says Ariella. 'Please? She can play with me while you look after Kit.' Ariella pauses. 'Because you know how tired you are, Mummy. You could get more sleep!'

I look at Ariella and almost laugh. Little minx knows which buttons to press all right. But it's a daft suggestion. Me? Stay here? Weirdly, though, her mother is watching me as though she's thinking about it.

'Can you clean?' she says sharply.

What? But I nod my head decisively. 'I'm really good at cleaning.' This is a bit of a stupid thing to say but the whole conversation is mad anyway.

'Any childcare experience?'

'I'm a very experienced babysitter. I used to look after my little brother all the time when my mum was at work.' What brother? 'And I used to do loads of babysitting back in Sheffield.' Also a lie. I'm annoyed with myself for letting slip where I come from, though.

The woman's face softens for a brief moment. 'Sheffield, eh? I went to uni there a long time ago . . .' She looks wistfully into the distance and then back at me.

'If you steal anything, or do anything you're not meant to, my husband will find you and you'll regret it. I can't pay you, but there's a spare room you can use. I can give you some clothes.' It's all delivered in a flat sort of monotone. Is she offering me a job?

She makes a frustrated noise. 'I want you to clean the house and help with Ariella. Understood?'

I blink a couple of times. I'm not sure I've exactly got much of a choice at the moment.

'Um, understood,' I say. I barely get my breath before Ariella has hurled herself at me, knocking the air out of my lungs and filling my mouth with her hair.

'We're going to have so much FUN!' she shrieks.

'I'm Charlotte,' says her mother with a tight little purse of her lips. 'I'll show you where the bathroom is in a minute. You look like you need a wash.'

I don't have time then to wonder what she meant about her husband. It doesn't occur to me then that farmers don't generally sound that scary.

Or to wonder why Charlotte would take a bleeding, dirty runaway into her house so readily.

Ariella doesn't let go of my hand or stop talking for a second as she leads me up a big staircase and along a landing flooded by a rare blast of sunshine. My feet sink into the thick carpeting. I'm suddenly hyper aware of my unwashed body. Funny, it didn't bother me when horses were my only housemates.

'We're going to *have so much fun!*' says Ariella again, and then, without drawing breath, 'And your bedroom is right

38

next to mine so I can come in and see you all the time!'

'Great,' I say with a forced smile. But she doesn't really notice as she leads me into a huge bathroom with white tiles and one of those old-fashioned claw-footed bathtubs, like I've seen on telly. Above the bath are glass shelves with all sorts of bottles of expensive-looking bubble bath. My fingers are itching to open them for a good sniff.

'Mummy says to give you a towel,' says Ariella and she opens the door of a wooden cabinet and extracts a huge armful of something soft, the same pale yellow colour as the walls.

Is that a thing people do? Buy towels to match their walls?

For a minute I'm so gobsmacked by this I stand uselessly in the middle of the room. Ariella finally stops talking and takes a breath.

'Are you all right, Kyla?' She says my name shyly, as though tasting the sound of it.

'Oh!' I say. 'Yeah, it's all good. It's nice in here.' Her eyebrows meet in a frown.

'It's just a *bathroom*,' she says. I picture the nasty green bath and sink in Zander's place. The blokes never lifted the seat when they peed and, like toddlers, they always left it all scuzzy. And there was always man hair everywhere.

Maybe it's just a bathroom to you, love, I think. *To me, it's heaven.*

Ariella doesn't shift and for a horrible second or two I

wonder if she thinks she's actually going to stay in here while I shower. So I purposefully take hold of her shoulders and march her out of the door.

'See you in a bit,' I say and before she can reply, I close the door in her face.

I stand with my back to it for a minute, looking around.

I don't really know why I'm here. Something feels a bit off about Charlotte and I don't know if it's just the dazed, sleep-deprived new-mother thing or something else. But I really need a shower. And I haven't got anywhere else to go. I decide I'll play it by ear for a few days and see what happens.

I'm just wondering about the whole having-a-shower-and-then-putting-filthy-clothes-back-on problem when there is a sharp knock at the door. I open it tentatively. Charlotte. Unsmiling, of course. She's holding a bundle of clothes on one arm. The baby is nestled into her neck like a little bug, her other hand almost covering his entire back.

'These should fit,' she says and hands me the clothes. There's a toothbrush and some deodorant resting on the top, along with a hairbrush that won't be any good for my hair. 'And do something about your face. There's ointment in the cabinet over the sink.'

'Thanks,' I say and attempt a smile that isn't returned. She gives me a crisp nod and turns away. I gently close the heavy wooden door again and place the clothes on a bench-seat.

I look around the huge bathroom, wondering if I have

finally caught a break. The showerhead is one of those metal rose ones as big as a dinner plate.

I stand under the hot water and let it run over my face, which hurts my cheek a bit. I don't know what it is about being in the shower, but the tears I thought were all finished come in a huge wave again, rocking me so hard I have to hold onto the wall with both hands, my head bowed, as the tears mix and fall with the hot water.

They're like a violent, sudden storm that passes over quickly and after a little while I reach for the most expensive-looking of the soaps and wash myself carefully, finding new cuts and bruises as I do. Once again I make a pledge to myself: the damage will stay on the *outside* from now on. Maybe if I say this enough, I can make it true.

It's only when I'm out of the shower and getting dried that I look properly at the clothes I've been given by Charlotte.

They're . . . nice. There's even underwear, including a bra a bit big for me. Hope I'm not going to have to shove a couple of socks in there.

The top is made from shimmery material that's so soft and light it's like holding cotton-wool balls in my hand. I pull it over my head. It's cut a bit lower than I'd like and I try to hoick it up a bit. There's a skirt too. I don't normally do skirts. This one is black and shiny and when I put it on, it clings to my hips in a way that makes me want to twirl in a right girly way. Maybe Ariella picked the clothes. Although they seem to be a bit sexy.

So who do they belong to? They're far too small to fit Charlotte, even before the baby. She's taller than me by about ten centimetres for a start.

There are no shoes so I just slip my own sneakers back on. They were in a load of stuff on one of Zander's recent raids on a clothing warehouse and are still in good nick, so I'm not too bothered about how they look.

Once I'm dressed I know I can't put it off any longer. I'm going to have to see what sort of state my face is in . . .

I wipe the steam clear from the big mirror over the sink and peer at it.

Looking back at me is a girl with raccoon shadows under too-big eyes. And the hair . . . I'm not even going there. Wincing, I turn my head this way and that to look at my cheek. A big circle of skin has been rubbed off and it looks about as sore as it feels. In fact, looking at it has made it hurt worse, like my brain has caught up with my eyes.

Charlotte told me to look in the cabinet so I open it up. There are the usual things people have. Tampons, cotton buds, some medicines. Quite a lot of medicines . . . Most of them seemed to be prescribed for Charlotte. She must rattle when she walks, judging by this lot. I don't bother trying to decode the labels. There are sterile wipes and antibiotic cream too, which I grab eagerly before smoothing some into the raw flesh. Behind a pack of normal plasters there's a small white box labelled SkinSavers. I open it up and peer inside. They look a bit like normal plasters but when I touch

42

one, it's slithery and strange under my fingers. I look closer at the box and make a face when I realise these are synthetic skin. I've heard about these. You slap them on and they grow into your own. Older women are starting to use them to cover up wrinkles and I saw someone in a magazine who'd done it so much, her body had reacted and it looked like she had a patchwork face. Yuck. They might have improved since then but a) I'm not taking the risk, b) they cost a bomb and I don't want Laughing Girl Charlotte to have any more reasons to kick me out and c) 'skin-coloured' is a laugh anyway, because they sure as hell don't match *my* skin. There's another pot of the magic cream there too, thankfully, so I dab some on, wincing at the pain.

I have one last glance around the bathroom to make sure I haven't left it in a state. Living with a bunch of blokes for ages might have made my standards slip. I try to look at it through Mum's eyes. I hang up my towel over the towel rail, which is on even though it's *summer*. Like I say, rich people are weird.

Then I hitch my top up one more time and open the door to the corridor.

I'm walking back towards the top of the stairs when I see a man coming up. I wait. He has his head down, reading something on his phone. He has thin gingery-yellow hair that's all sort of swept up at the front and his bulbous nose and cheeks are the colour of uncooked bacon. He's fat but not that tall and I hear him wheezing as he reaches the top.

I stand still, not sure what to do with myself. He looks up sharply in surprise then draws his head back as he regards me. His eyes seem to scuttle up and down the entire length of my body like bugs. His tongue runs over his bottom lip, leaving it glistening, and a slow smile creeps across his face. I find myself pulling self-consciously at the top again.

'So you're our runaway then,' he says in a flat, nasally voice. 'Kylie, isn't it?'

'Kyla,' I say. I know I should do something to make myself seem friendly but I can't do it. He's obviously a total creep. If I was a cat, I'd be arching my back and hissing right now. Maybe it's obvious how I'm feeling, because his eyes stay cold and flat. This makes me think of sharks.

'Well, make sure you keep your nose clean,' he says. 'The last one was a light-fingered little cow.'

The last one? Mystery owner of the clingy clothes, I presume.

But I try to smile in a reassuring way. 'I promise I'll do my job well. And, um, thanks for letting me stay.'

The eyes go wandering again and I blush, but it's more to do with anger than embarrassment. He nods distractedly and looks down at his phone again. We have to pass each other. The corridor is wide enough for both of us but he manages to brush close enough for me to smell sweat and cigar smoke.

I make a mental note to stay out of his way.

CHAPTER 5

question marks

Ariella is chattering away about something as I load the dishwasher. I've got a system now for doing it so Miss Picky-Pants Charlotte doesn't complain.

Mum never had one so this is one of the many things I've had to learn to do in the last few weeks, along with making tea and coffee for Charlotte, boiling eggs and making Marmite toast for Ariella, who doesn't appear to eat anything else, and cleaning this massive house.

I can't really believe I'm still here.

A few days after I agreed to stay, I woke in the middle of the night, heart thumping, covered in sweat and shaking all over. A bad dream? I'd already forgotten it but the lingering fear still clung to me. I started to make sense of where I was but it was so dark I felt like I'd suffocate from it. I began to panic then as a million unwanted thoughts started to batter me.

What was I even *doing* here? I'm no au pair. All I knew how to do was thieve. So why didn't I just take what I could and . . . leave? I even got out of bed and started to get dressed.

It was as I was pulling on the second sock that I slowed down and began to think properly about what I was doing. I had nowhere to go. And much as I like to think I'm tough, I've never been alone on the streets before. I always had Jax, even if I was taking care of him as much as he took care of me. Let's face it, I had a bed here. I had food. I had shelter.

Ariella's face came into my mind then. I thought about the way she'd sometimes sidle up and lean against me with her hot, solid little body. Completely trusting. I moved away when she did that. I don't want to get too attached. Even if I wasn't going to disappear in the middle of *this* night, I reserved the right to do it on another.

I glance over at her now. Half-listening to her stream-of-consciousness rabbiting is another skill I've had to work on. I learned my lesson about mindlessly saying, 'Mmm, yeah, mmm . . .' when I realised she'd asked me if I could kill someone with my bare hands. The constant questions ('What's your favourite sort of crisp?' 'Do cats like cherries?' and 'If the world is spinning all the time, how come we don't fall off?' being a few examples) nearly drove me nuts in the first couple of days. I sort of got an inkling why her mum looks so shell-shocked, especially as she doesn't appear to sleep, like, ever.

I have only seen creepy Mick two or three times. He's

away a lot and doesn't seem much like a farmer to me. There's a secretive air about him when he's here and he always closes doors before speaking on the phone. He hasn't crossed any lines with me anyway, despite my initial impressions. Apart from when he took a glass from me and deliberately let his hand linger on mine, he has mainly just given me sleazy looks. I can handle him, I think. As long as it's just his eyes that stray.

I don't want to know what happened to the last au pair. I have to get through one day at a time at the moment and hope for the best. I've told them I'm seventeen and they seem to believe me. I passed my fifteenth birthday huddled in the corner of the small box room I'm staying in, arms around my knees, grieving for Mum, for Jax and for Cal. But it's getting easier every day. When I find myself being a bit soft about Ariella, I make myself think about something else. Like the fact that she has no real connection to me. She's not my family. I have no family. There's only me now. And it's going to stay that way.

My attention drifts back to her as I put away the last plate.

'. . . and Brutus got mud all over Maddie's dress and she shouted!' says Ariella at the kitchen table.

'Oh, really?' I say and idly go over to switch on the radio. Then I look at her.

'Who's Maddie?' I say, trying to look interested. Ariella can get in a strop if I forget the names of any of her many school friends, although I've noticed she doesn't ever seem to get invited to anyone's house, despite it being the school holidays. I've been told all about her older half-brothers that live in London and how 'Daddy' used to be married to someone else. Anyway, I don't recognise this name.

Ariella flashes me that sly look of hers.

'Maddie was my friend,' she says, lashes lowered. 'She helped us, like you do. But Mummy said she had to go away and there was lots of shouting.'

A chill creeps along my bare arms. I'm in a sort of halter-top dress today. It's light blue, covered in brown spots. I know it suits me but it's far too posh to be wearing to clean a house. Everything I've been given is too posh for that but I don't feel like I can say anything. Charlotte seems to want me to be dressed like this. Mad.

I rub my arms. Ariella watches me. 'You look pretty in her dress but not as pretty as Maddie did.'

I let out a loud laugh. She cracks me up sometimes with her blunt, kiddy honesty. But I want to know what happened with this Maddie person. I'm guessing she is the 'thieving little cow' Mick referred to before.

Charlotte appears quite suddenly then at the doorway. Kit is in the sling, quiet for once. I've been dreading that she will ask me to change him or do anything at all baby-related. But she keeps him close to her all the time. She has never once smiled at me in the entire time I've been here.

'Why don't you go and watch telly, Ariella,' she says flatly. Ariella obediently gets up and, shooting me a look I can't read, trots off to the entertainment room at the back of the house. It's like a small cinema. They all spend a lot of time in there. Going outside isn't an option at the moment because the rains have come back.

All the lights are on but the grey gloom seeps into the kitchen. The rains started again a week ago and since then there hasn't been a let-up. I heard on the radio that they're running out of places for flood refugees and am glad we're nowhere near a river here. I arrange my face into something friendly and look up to see that Charlotte is staring at me. Her eyes are puffy and her skin is a sort of pale yellow in this light. She looks awful.

I smile weakly and she turns her attention to the baby, who has started to grizzle.

She says, 'Can you make me some tea.' It's like her sentences are too knackered to bother with question marks. She unhooks the sling and then starts grappling with one of her enormous veiny footballs. I busy myself with the kettle.

'My husband's coming home today,' she says. I can't explain it but this seems to hang in the air, waiting for someone to catch it. I put the filled kettle on the base and clear my throat.

'Is there anything you want doing, then?' I say. I get out her favourite mug and place a teabag in it before turning to look at her. Her head is down, her eyes on the baby sucking noisily away.

'No,' she says quietly. 'But he has an old friend staying tomorrow. You should keep Ariella out of the way.'

'OK,' I say quietly, placing the mug of tea in front of her. On a mat, of course. Even though the place was a total tip when I got here, she's gone overboard now on tidiness. I've learned my lesson about stuff like using a mat for hot drinks, or leaving anything lying about. She had a right go at me about 'standards' not long after I got here.

'I'll go and see what Ariella's up to,' I say and leave the room, grateful to get away from Charlotte's pinched old face. She doesn't respond. It's possible she's fallen asleep. I once came in when her head was lolling and a thread of dribble was hanging from her lip. Her eyes almost shrivelled me up when she came to and saw me standing there.

Walking down the hallway towards the entertainment room, I stop, noticing a picture on a table there for the first time. The photos in the house are mostly of Ariella or Mick surfing, horse riding or holding a gun and some sort of dead animal by the tail. This one is in a plain, brown frame, unlike the others, which are framed in heavy-looking gold or silver.

I peer down at it. It's Charlotte. She doesn't look that much older than me here. She's sitting on a rock, wearing a bikini top and a pair of shorts, smiling into the camera. Her shining hair hangs around her shoulders in a way I'd kill for and she's much slimmer than now. She's so much prettier too but it's not just that which is so different. It's like she's properly alive.

She looks like a person who has lots of question marks in her sentences.

Looking at the picture makes me even more determined not to have kids, if that's what it does to you.

I'm making Ariella's tea later when I hear her shout, 'Dadeeeeee!' I reflexively yank the neckline of the dress up and start buttering her toast soldiers.

He comes into the kitchen carrying Ariella upside down. She giggles hysterically as he turns her over onto her feet. His face glows red from the exertion, and his small, pale eyes immediately run up and down the length of my body. *Creep*. I briefly picture kneeing him in the groin.

'Ah, it's the delightful Kylie,' he says. I've told him my name twice now. I think he does it to wind me up, so I don't give him the satisfaction of correcting him. I fail to crank my lips into any kind of smile.

'Ariella, your tea's ready,' I say, putting her Gomez plate down on her Gomez mat. She's obsessed with that damn rat.

No one ever told me how I should address Charlotte and Mick so I avoid using their names. 'Can I get you something to drink?' I say to him.

'I can get myself a beer,' he says, smiling and showing his small white teeth. He reminds me of a fat rodent. 'Would you like one too?' he says.

'Um, no thank you.' I can only imagine how that would go down with Charlotte.

'Ariella, your tea,' I remind her. She's looking adoringly at her dad, who moves to the fridge and pulls out a bottle of the posh beer he likes. He looks me square in the eye as he removes the top with his hand. I think I'm meant to be impressed by this and have to stop myself from laughing at the idiot man.

'I don't want that smelly egg,' says Ariella. 'I want pizza for my tea instead.' Two days ago she told me that she would never eat pizza because the 'cheese is all shiny'. Now her gaze shuttles between me and her dad and I sense a weird play for attention going on here.

I'm about to take her on because I know Charlotte would never stand for this. Then I see the smile on Mick's face. 'My baby knows what she likes, just like her dad,' he says. Ariella beams. 'Better get cracking, hadn't you? You can do one for me an' all.'

Ariella sits at the table and dramatically pushes away the plate. The egg topples sadly from the egg cup and rolls on the table, leaving a trail of yellow yolk, like innards.

Without speaking, I clean it up, keeping my eyes lowered so neither of them can see the treachery in my eyes. I'm picturing throwing the whole plate at the wall and walking out.

I'm at the sink when I feel Mick move behind me. He reaches past to fill a cup of water, close enough for me to feel his hot breath on my cheek. When the cup is full he slides his hand along my waist and down my hip. I freeze. Now I'm picturing turning round and bringing my elbow into his face. Hard.

'Hurry up with that pizza, eh, darling? I don't like to be

kept waiting,' he whispers. I *somehow* manage not to do anything violent. He goes back to the table. That's when I see Charlotte in the doorway, as still and shadowy as a ghost. I don't know how long she's been there. I catch my breath, ready to launch into my defence, but she quickly looks away and comes over to kiss Mick on the cheek before sliding into a chair opposite him.

I open the freezer and take out a pizza, my hands shaking hard so that I fumble and almost drop it. I'm wondering just what kind of weird house I'm living in as I open the packaging. I rip it a bit more than necessary to open it.

CHAPTER 6

dangerous beasts

As soon as Ariella is in bed I go to my room and watch the telly in there all evening, although I can't even tell you which programmes I watch. I'm too worried about how I'm going to cope with old octopus hands without punching him in the face. I'd never have stood for that kind of crap before. One of Zander's brothers stayed once and tried it on with me. He lost two teeth. Luckily, Zander thought it was the funniest thing ever.

It's the element of surprise, you see. No one expects a skinny girl to hit them so I get in there first. It's something Jax taught me, learned over many years of dealing with bullies.

Oh, mate. I miss you so much.

In the middle of the night I wake up, heart pounding. For a

second I think someone is in the room. Pearly moonlight slices through the gap in the curtains. There's just enough light for me to see that I'm alone.

I swing my legs out of bed and run across to the door to check it's still locked.

I knew I wouldn't have forgotten to do it. A bad dream, then? My heart's still banging as I cross the floor and get back into bed. Shivering, I pull the duvet around my shoulders.

About a second later, the door handle wiggles. Someone is turning it from the outside. I'm sitting bolt upright, clutching the duvet up to my chin.

I'm out of bed and across the room, ready to let fly at the sleazy creep behind the door. I'm mentally packing my stuff as I unlock it and fling it open.

Ariella is standing there in her pink PJs, shivering all over. In her arm she's holding her fluffy rat toy.

'What is it?' Relief makes me hiss like a popped balloon.

Her big eyes shine in the dim glow of the night-light outside my door.

'I can't sleep,' she says, too loud for this hour of the night. 'Mummy and Daddy were fighting and then Mummy cried. Can I sleep with you?'

I hesitate for a second and then sigh, resigned.

'Come on, then,' I say. 'But no hogging the duvet. Or talking. Or putting cold feet on me.'

She pushes past me to get to the bed. I poke my head out of the door and listen but can't hear anything.

Shivering, I lock the door before climbing into bed. Ariella curls around me and something hurts inside, like pressure on a bruise. A tender feeling presses on my chest as her breathing slows into sleepiness. After a few moments, I roll away into a chilled corner of the bed, alone. I can't get too close. Anyone I've ever cared about has been taken from me. That's just the way it is. If I'm going to survive then it has to be on my terms. And there can be no passengers.

The next day Charlotte makes me clean the house from top to bottom, even though it doesn't really need it. She's even more brittle and snappy than usual. At midday a woman arrives with various bags and she's all smiles then. They disappear off upstairs together.

Various cars and vans arrive and the kitchen fills up with people cooking and shouting orders to each other. Women with towering displays of fresh flowers shout, "Scuse me!' as they jostle past and arrange them on gleaming surfaces. I peek in at the dining room and see it has been laid out as if for a banquet. Ariella is chatty and hyped up and it's hard not to let a little of the excitement rub off.

When Charlotte emerges later, she's had her hair done so that it swings, shiny and smooth, around her face. She's wearing make-up that hides the purple shadows under her eyes and is dressed in a black clingy dress and shoes with killer heels.

I say, 'Wow, you look great,' and she purses her scarlet-lipsticked lips in a way that's almost threatening to be a smile.

'Who's coming?' I say, pushing my luck. She closes up so fast I almost hear the snap.

'Old school friend of my husband,' she says tightly. 'But he's an important man. Just make sure you and Ariella stay out of the way.'

I turn and make a rude face as she tip-taps out of the room.

Ariella's in the bath later when I hear raised voices and laughter. I go to the bathroom window, which looks out over the gravel driveway at the front of the house.

There are three large black cars with darkened windows. Each one has the distinctive number plate of the Counterinsurgency Squads. A tremor of worry ripples through me. CATS? Why are they coming here? I have to remind myself that now Cal has gone I have no more to fear than any other citizen. They have no way of knowing I was in that Torch house.

I squeeze my eyes shut, thinking about the explosion again. I hope they didn't know what was going on. That the end came quickly . . .

'Are you crying?'

I come back to myself. Ariella has made a beard out of bath foam. She peers at me through the bubbles.

'No, course not,' I say, with a strangled cough. 'Come on, let's get you dry before you end up wrinkled like an old prune.'

Giggling, she gets up, covering most of the floor in soapy water.

I'm combing out her damp hair when my curiosity takes over.

'So who's this special guest coming tonight, then?' I say.

Ariella looks sideways at me with wide eyes. 'Daddy says he is a big cat and I asked him if he meant like a tiger. And then he *laughed*,' she says, very seriously. 'But I don't think it's funny because tigers eat people, don't they, Kyla?'

I try to give her a reassuring smile. 'Don't worry,' I say, 'he's not a real tiger. He's just a man. Daddy was making a joke.' *He's a right comedian, your dad.*

Satisfied, she pops her thumb into her mouth.

I'm thinking about this visitor. He might not be a real tiger. But that doesn't mean he isn't dangerous.

I do exactly what Charlotte says and keep out of the way for the evening. When Ariella is safely tucked up in bed, I scoot into the kitchen and grab some chicken from the fridge, some crisps and an apple to take up to my room. I can hear loud voices and laughter coming from the dining room. I rush past.

Going up the stairs I glance out of the window and see two men in CATS uniform standing in front of the house. They both have assault rifles slung across their chests.

Whoever this visitor is, he's someone important. I stand back from the window, feeling uneasy.

I've been at Craydale Farm for a couple of months now. My

cheek has healed and although the bad memories still chase me, I'm getting stronger by the day. I like Ariella, even though I won't let myself love her. But I'm not ready to move on.

I like being under the radar.

But what if I've been kidding myself that I'm safe here?

CHAPTER 7

electricity

I go to bed early but can't shut off my mind. Worries about staying here seem to roll through my head constantly. And I keep thinking about Jax and Cal.

I keep wondering why Mick has got some CATS boss on a sleepover too. Even though I'm not wanted for anything specific, I don't really know if I'm on any kind of security list. And, let's face it, when I lived with Zander I spent my time taking part in robberies. Maybe my face was caught by a buzz drone.

It's after two a.m. when I decide I need to go and get some water. In the past I'd have thought nothing of getting it from the bathroom tap. But I've got fussy since I've been here, I guess. All the flooding has done something to the reservoirs and now they're saying you should only drink water from certain taps, like the one in the kitchen here.

I don't have a dressing gown so I pull on a cardigan over my nightie and step into one of the longer skirts I've been given for a bit of warmth. Surely no one will be up to see my weird outfit anyway.

I pad carefully down the stairs and stop abruptly when I see the shadow of one of the guards against the front door. He's not moving and I wonder if he's sleeping on his feet, like a penguin. I would have laughed at this but my teeth are chattering with nerves in the chill night air.

The house is quiet, apart from the tick-tocking of the grandfather clock that sits at the bend in the staircase and the odd pipe banging. My own heartbeat seems loud in my ears as I push open the kitchen door and hurry over to the sink.

The only light comes from the displays of the cooker, microwave and dishwasher. That suits me fine. I'll grab a glass of water and leg it back to my room.

I get a tall glass from the cupboard over the sink and fill it with water. I take a greedy gulp and then a sound behind me seems to tip it from my grasp. The glass smashes into the sink. I spin round. Mick sits at the nearest end of the table. It's too dim to see him clearly but I can make out the shine of his eyes.

'Oh dear, bit clumsy, are we? Bit of a butterfingers?' he slurs.

He gets up unsteadily. He's drunk as anything and not tall, but he's fat and much, much stronger than me. I try to sound confident.

'I'm sorry. I'll clear it up.' I pick up the biggest piece of glass and stand up, ready to get the dustpan and brush from the cupboard across the way.

He's standing less than a metre away from me now.

'You better had, hadn't you?' he says in a low hiss. 'You're an ungrateful little bitch, aren't you? We let you into our home and you think you can damage our property, is that it?'

He moves fast, so fast I don't get time to react. His hand is up against my throat, pushing me back against the sink. His other hand is on my leg. It's hot, sweaty, disgusting. I can hear his rapid breathing, see the too-big pupils in his glazed eyes. 'I expect we can work something out, though, hmm?' he says. The smell of cigars and whiskey makes me want to gag.

'Let me go,' I say through gritted teeth.

He leers, showing teeth stained with something. Red wine? I don't know. It reminds me of blood.

'Where would you go, little runaway Kylie?' he says in a quiet, silky voice. 'No one is missing *you*, are they? In a bit of trouble, are we? Is that why we found you, all scratched up in the barn, eh?' His breathing has got faster now and he's pushing the weight of his body against me. I can't move at all. 'We help each other out around here,' he says now. 'You get to stay in my house and enjoy my hospitality. My baby girl likes you. The wife likes you. Well, as much as she ever likes anyone. I like you too. All you have to do is be a bit more friendly, eh?'

His red, sweaty face looms in close and his hand wanders up my thigh. Everything shrinks inside. Disgust crawls over my skin like biting ants and then my anger expands outwards, filling me up.

I spit. It hits his cheek and slides down his face. There's a hitch in time, like neither of us can believe what I just did. His eyes widen in shock. My head snaps to the side. I didn't even see his hand move. My hearing's gone all muffled and funny and I'm dizzy. He grabs my throat, muttering, squeezing so I can feel myself starting to black out. His wet fish lips touch mine and sick rises inside. *No. No. I won't let this happen.*

I reach behind, fumbling for something, anything I can use to make this stop.

They close around the heavy bottom of the broken glass. I swing it round and it catches the side of his face. A crimson gash opens like he's been unzipped. He roars with pain and clutches his face, stepping back. His eyes bulge with hate as he swings a punch. I duck and he almost topples over.

Got to get out of here! I shove him, hard, in the chest and he stumbles backwards, still roaring. I can feel the energy of a waking house as I run out of the kitchen and towards the front door.

'What the hell is happening here?'

The commanding voice stops me in my tracks. I turn round. A big man with glasses is tying a navy blue dressing gown around his middle. The glasses glint and I can't see his eyes.

Mick stumbles out of the kitchen. Blood drips from the fingers clamped to his face.

'Little thief!' he yells. 'She's the au pair, Alex! I caught her going through my wallet and she attacked me!'

Two large bodies seem to appear from nowhere behind me. From the corner of my eye I see starched blue uniforms and smell the damp night air on them.

'He's a filthy liar!' I yell. 'He attacked me! I was defending myself!'

'Why, you little . . .' Mick lurches forward again and I know he's going to hit me. I step backwards but feel strong hands gripping my upper arms. I cringe away from the blow, turning my face the other way. But it doesn't come. Panic pushes my breath out in fast pants. I look back and see the other bloke has one hand lightly on Mick's shoulder. Mick is looking at him and then back at me.

'How many times have I told you,' says the other man in an icy voice, 'that you are to call me Alexander? We're not students any more.' He turns to look at Mick, who has a cringing expression on his face. 'Hmm?'

'Sorry, I, um —' says Mick but 'Alexander' cuts him off. 'I think one of my men should drive you to hospital to get this . . .' he gestures vaguely in the direction of Mick's bleeding face, 'stitched up.'

Mick nods, looking as pathetic as a kicked dog. The other man turns away. 'Now I'm going back to bed. I have an early start in the morning.' He throws his voice to the men behind me. 'As for *that*. You can lock her up. We'll drop her off at a police station in the morning and they can deal with her.'

Alexander starts to walk up the stairs. One of the CATS men releases my arm and moves towards Mick.

All I can hear is the word '*that*' in my head. Like I'm a bit of dirt that must be scraped off and disposed of quickly. The rage explodes again. Hot and clean, like a fire that will melt them all to ashes.

Mick and the other guy disappear into the kitchen. The one holding my arm says, 'Come on then, you,' in a weary, disgusted tone. I feel the grip on my arm loosen for a second.

I don't even think. My body is pure movement. I swing my arm up at the elbow and feel a crunch as my fist makes contact with the guard's nose. He cries out and goes to grab me but I lift my knee and ram it into his groin. He crumples like he's been shot, groaning. I start to run down the hallway but the other guard is almost on top of me straight away. I jab at his eyes and he pulls back so that I can swing my foot round and smash it into his chest, winding him. I'm almost there . . . almost at the door. A crazy urge to laugh bubbles up inside. Freedom!

And then pain shrieks through every part of my body, fizzing, frying me with hot agony. Crying out, I fall onto the ground and huddle into a ball. Another wave slams into me. I bare my teeth like an animal and the warmth around my legs tells me I've wet myself.

'That's enough,' says a voice somewhere distant. 'You've made your point. Throw her in the van and we'll deal with her tomorrow.'

I'm lifted up roughly under the arms. My head lolls. The sharp slap around my face barely registers, nor the hissed, angry words that tumble, hot, into my ear.

'Little cow. There will be more of that if you try anything else.'

They throw me into the back of a van. My head throbs in waves that seem to expand then shrink tight into a pinprick. My clothes are damp and cold and I'm suddenly ashamed about wetting myself. I pull a rough sheet of material around me and lie there, shivering. I know that I have to try to lie still. I'll feel better if I just give it time, I tell myself.

I've never been volted before. Zander had, more than once. Used to boast that they needed to use a more powerful volter on him because he was 'resistant' or something.

God, I'm practically missing Zander. This is so messed up.

Bastards . . .

Self-pitying tears rise up inside and I squeeze my eyes shut.

What's going to happen to me now?

I'm so cold. I can feel myself shuddering against the hard floor of the van. A headache rattles around my skull and my wet skirt clings to my legs, rubbing them sore. I can hear the rain outside, drumming onto the roof of the van. My wrists and legs are tied with some sort of strong, stretchy stuff. I try to bite it but it hurts my teeth. I can only move my hands and feet a little way apart. If I try to stretch the binding further, it shrinks, so I stop.

Somehow, despite all this, I drop off to a muddled sleep.

I'm jolted awake when the doors of the van open and daylight blasts in. I crack my swollen eyelids open. The events of the night before fill my mind and I go limp with fear.

The rain falls warm onto me as they drag me from the van. I'm so thirsty. I never even got my glass of water last night. I let the rain run into my mouth, even though it has all sorts in it, they say. The guards from yesterday jerk me roughly as they carry me towards a massive black car. One of them whispers an obscene thing into my ear. I wince at his sour breath. He has a piece of gauze strapped across his nose and I want to laugh that someone of my size could do that to a thumping great man, but I think he'll hit me if I do so I lower my eyes, meek as a lamb.

Lamb of God, have mercy on us . . .

I remember Mum saying that prayer when I was small. I believed her when she said prayers protect you.

My bound feet drag behind me, churning up mud, and then I'm thrown into the back of the black car. A sheet of plastic has been put over the seats and as the door is closed behind me, I look around and see that man Alexander from last night, looking at me with a wrinkled nose, like I smell. I *do* smell.

He turns away and looks out of the other window. The windows are tinted, so the greyness outside is deepened and intensified.

The next thing I know, he's holding up a phone.

My phone. And the screen is filled with the picture of Cal.

Oh, God . . .

'Who is this?' he snaps.

I swallow, trying to keep my eyes completely blank.

'No idea,' I say in the boldest voice I can.

'Isn't this your device?' he says crisply. He has a weirdly womanly mouth with a bow-shaped upper lip.

'No.'

This seems to surprise him because he pauses before speaking again. I force myself to wait.

'Why was it in your possession then?'

I roll my eyes, hoping this isn't overdoing it. 'Because I stole it, didn't I?' I say, as though he is the stupidest man alive.

I got that phone recently. I only texted Jax from it and I never sign off texts. I didn't use the email. There wasn't time for anything much before my life fell apart. There's only one photo on there. Why did I take that photo? I haven't even been able to bring myself to look at it since then so it had no purpose. And now it might get me into even more trouble than I'm already in. Cal escaped from the Facility but he's dead now. Still, I can't let them know there was any connection between us.

I risk speaking again. 'Didn't your old mucker Mick tell you I was a dirty little thief? That was right after he tried to rape me. You might remember.'

A muscle in Alexander's cheek tightens and I'm

frightened I've gone too far. I shrink back against the door like a kicked dog, expecting a blow.

But the man next to me just gives a loud sigh. 'This is a convenient place to stay sometimes,' he says through tight lips. I notice they are completely without colour and seem to blend into his face. 'He's no friend of mine, whatever he thinks.' He pauses and then his voice is sharp and full of authority again. 'So where did you get the phone?'

'I lifted it from some lad's pocket in Sheffield. We were in a crowd. It was easy.' I shrug, praying that I'm putting on a convincing act.

A long silence fills the car. I can feel my heart stampeding in my chest but force myself to look into his eyes. Or, at least, where they lurk behind those glasses.

Finally he says, 'You're quite something, aren't you, young Kyla? Thief. Vicious little wildcat. A devil with the face of an angel.'

This makes me look down at last, heat creeping up my face. Is that what I am? I don't like that description. That's not who I want to be.

But he's speaking again.

'I have a proposition for you. I'm not interested in debating its pros and cons. You either take it or you don't, I really don't care.' He pauses and then turns to me. His eyes behind those shiny lenses are still hard to see and I realise the glasses are tiny screens. He's probably reading emails and surfing for holidays or something while he's talking to me.

Or arranging for some people to be arrested. Of course he is. Why would he waste time even looking at someone as worthless as me?

'Do you understand?' he says.

I find myself nodding. He has that sort of voice. Cold and low and assuming you will do what it says, always.

'So, *Kyla*.' He says my name silkily, stretching it out in a way that makes me shiver uncomfortably. Then his voice changes, becomes hard, businesslike. 'I'm arresting you for three counts of assault, including wounding with intent using a deadly weapon. You have the right . . . *blah blah*.' He waves his hand and then sighs deeply. 'You will be tried. Eventually. But the courts have a backlog so I doubt you will see the inside of a witness box for at least two years. And in the meantime you will be spending time in a young offender's institution. It's called the Facility. Have you ever heard of it?'

My mouth somehow goes even drier. I can't reply. I thought the Facility had been closed down after what happened with Cal and the riots. But maybe it's open again. And maybe the experiments have started up again. I think about punching him and trying to get out of the car but I know the doors will be locked. And I'd never get away.

I hang my head, suddenly so tired that I wish I could sleep and never wake up. I could be with Mum, Jax and Cal. Somewhere better than here. It doesn't seem as though there is anything much to live for any more. I glance back at the house, hoping Ariella isn't upset. I wonder what they've told her?

The man is speaking again.

'Or, there is an alternative,' he says. My head shoots up. I don't know what to say. Is he going to let me go? Then it strikes me maybe he's a creep like Mick. I set my jaw and beam what I think of him with my eyes. Never. He'd have to kill me first.

He laughs and it's a surprising sound. A proper laugh, filled with humour, like someone has just told him a joke.

'Don't flatter yourself, darling! Anyway, I'm not interested in children. But there it is again!' he says, and leans over, taking my chin in his hand. It hurts and my eyes water. 'That spark . . .' It's like he's having some sort of conversation with himself, the weirdo.

He lets go of my chin and his face is serious and unreadable again. The glasses suddenly clear and reveal his eyes, which are pale green and piggy with a red, exhausted tinge.

'We need more young people – young women, specifically – to be trained up for security work,' he says. 'We send them to one of our training centres.'

'What kind of security work? What would I have to do?' My voice croaks now and I have to cough.

He knocks on a glass pane separating the front of the car from the back, which slides open a little. He says, 'Water' and a bottle of water is handed back, glistening with cold. I want to snatch it but wait until he takes off the lid. I grab it between my bound hands. As I pour the sweet water into my mouth, I'm filled with gratitude. I almost love him for giving me the water.

'Better?' he says after a moment and I nod.

'Thank you,' I force myself to say.

'Just security work,' he goes on. I'd forgotten my question and am confused for a minute. I suddenly feel conscious of how dirty I am and want to shrink into myself again.

'You might not even get that far, so there's no point discussing it now,' he continues. 'Many recruits don't make it through the basic training. It needs a certain . . . strength of mind and spirit, shall we say. You may not even last a day.'

I stare into his eyes as though I'll find an answer there but they are blank and unseeing, almost as though his thoughts are somewhere else entirely. I clear my throat before speaking.

'And if I say I don't want to do it?'

He sighs again and glances at the gold watch on his pale wrist like this is all so *boring*. He has small, neat hands that are weirdly creepy on a man of his age. 'Well, you will go to prison and await your trial,' he says wearily. 'That's if you're still alive.'

I swallow some more water and look away from him, desperately trying to think. What should I do? My whole future rests on what I decide here. Should I take my chances with an arrest?

I think about Cal then, when he told me and Jax about the Facility. He tried to look cool, but I saw the way he clenched his fists so that his knuckles strained white. It made me want to hold his hand but I didn't. I wish I had now. He kept swallowing too, like the words were hard to force out. He said he'd do anything not to go back to the place where they experimented on him and stole his identity. I shudder at the thought. I can't do it.

But what's this 'training' all about? Will I become some sort of cool ninja spy at the end of it? It can't be that easy. What do they do to you at these training centres? I don't like what he said about 'surviving'.

Then I remember that surviving is something I seem to be good at. The pig flu didn't get me. CATS didn't get me when they picked up Jax and killed him. And the farmhouse was blown to bits with everyone inside, apart from me.

I survive even when I don't want to, it feels like. Maybe I can get through this too.

I wipe my mouth awkwardly with the back of my wrist and try to sit up straighter in the seat, despite how small and cold and frightened I feel.

'All right,' I say and my trembling voice gives me away. 'I'll do it.'

I lift my chin defiantly.

I have no clue what I have just agreed to.

CHAPTER 8

road trip

The car door opens and I'm yanked out by the arm. Alexander doesn't even look at me as I stumble out of the seat, my bound ankles dragging behind me. He has probably already disappeared behind his screens and is onto the next problem that must be dealt with.

'There'd better not be a peep out of you, missy,' hisses the guard as he frogmarches me back to the van. 'I'd like nothing better than to give you the hiding you deserve so you'd better not give me any excuse at all – are we clear?'

I nod, meek again. The rain has stopped briefly and the air smells sweet and clean. He opens the back of the van and just as he's about to throw me inside, I glance up at the house. Charlotte is standing at a window on the first floor, the baby against her chest and one of her hands splayed on the back of his tiny head. Our eyes meet. It's impossible to read her expression but, despite everything, despite the fact that I am sore, cold, hungry, and I smell of wee and shame, I wouldn't want her life. I wish I could say goodbye to Ariella but the coward in me knows it's better this way. I don't want even her to see me like this.

But I'm not to be let off that easily.

I pull my legs up and huddle in the back of the van. The guard is about to close the doors when I hear a high-pitched wail coming from the direction of the house and suddenly she's there, a whirlwind in PJs and bare feet.

'*Kylaaaaaaa!*' she calls desperately. Pleading.

I can't do it. I'm not strong enough. I can't make her feel better. I don't know how to make anyone feel better. And anyway it's not my job any more, is it? I hurriedly reach over and pull one of the doors myself as the guard slams the other with a loud thunk. I can still hear her calling as the engine starts. I curl into a ball on the cold, metal floor and try to will the sound away as the van begins to move. But her voice tears at me inside long after we've driven away. I didn't get too close to her, just as I'd promised myself. But I got close enough to feel guilty about leaving her behind with no explanation. Next time I'll be harder still. I won't let anyone in.

I thought I'd get treated a little better after the conversation with Mr Big Cheese Alexander, and agreed to go on his security course or whatever it is. I didn't expect to get loaded back into this van like I'm not even human.

I want to wash and change my clothes more than anything in the world, even more than I want some more water and to eat something. I'm starving, even though my stomach's all in knots as I wonder about what's going to happen next.

I lose track of time a bit but I suppose it's about an hour before the engine sounds change and the van slows to a stop. It seems ages before the doors are thrown open again. I flinch and tuck into myself tighter when I see the face of the guard. He still hates me. I guess hard blokes like him don't take kindly to being half beaten up by skinny girls like me. Serves him right. I avoid his eye anyway because I'm not stupid. No point in winding him up further.

'Get out,' he orders and I sit up and edge towards the open doors. I lower my legs out and shuffle down, looking around. There's a high, barbed-wire fence and a massive gate behind us. Two soldiers guard it, their expressions stony. In front of me is a low, red-brick building. I don't get the chance to see any more of it because the guard takes my arm again and drags me towards a building off to the side of the main one. I crane my neck to look behind me and see a bunch of soldiers marching in formation, their feet crunching in time through gravel.

My biggest fan shoves me into the building, which is a sort of long hut. Inside it's like a changing room with rows of benches and a stone floor. I have a dim memory of when I went to school and had PE, a lifetime ago.

'Clean yourself up. Change your clothes. You're disgusting,' barks Fan Boy, wrinkling his nose. I hate him for saying this. I'd like to break his nose all over again. 'Oh, and,' he's leering now, 'these aren't women's changing rooms so you'd better be quick. About fifty squaddies are about to use these facilities in five minutes.'

He goes to a locker, laughing, and pulls out some faded green trousers and a shirt. They're army clothes made for a man and they're going to swamp me, but anything clean and dry would be welcome about now. He does something to the bindings on my wrists and ankles. My arms flop free and then I move to catch the clothes he throws at my face.

'Five minutes.' He sits down on one of the benches and stares at me. 'Well, get moving then.'

I hurry through to the showers, praying for cubicles, but no, there's just rows of shower-heads and a long trough. Shivering and looking all around, I peel off the wet clothes, praying no one will come in. The water is hot and even though there's no soap, I quickly sluice myself down, grateful to be getting clean. I'm in there for all of three minutes and then stand shivering, realising I have no towel. I have to use the top I was wearing to dry myself, all the while so terrified about people coming in that my teeth grind together and my hands shake when I try to do up buttons on the huge shirt.

I have to roll the sleeves up several times and the trouser legs too, but the clothes are dry and clean and the relief is huge. It's like all my needs are waiting in line because as

77

soon as I feel this I remember the thirst and hunger gnawing at me inside.

There's a bin and I stuff my other clothes in there. They were never mine, anyway. I had plenty to wear when Jax and I lived at Zander's place. Never thought anything of chucking something away because it had a tiny tear or stain. For a minute I picture my favourite top, shimmery sky-blue and made from that special material that adapts to your temperature and changes colour in different lights. Thinking Fabric, they call it. Tears fill my eyes and I think, *What, so you're missing a bloody top now? Get a grip, girl.* But it's not the top, not really. It's the thought of having something of my own, even if it only came from thieving. Like I had some sort of control over my own life. I wipe my hand across my face and push hair out of my eyes. I slide my feet into my sneakers, stand up straight and push my shoulders back before walking back to where Fan Boy is waiting.

He laughs unkindly and shakes his head as though he's never seen anything more disgusting than me. He has small, watery blue eyes and his teeth have the distinctive blueish tinge of whitening tablets that have gone wrong. Who'd have thought a big thug like him would try to change his appearance? His nose is all swollen and smushed looking.

Ha! Serves you right, you pathetic bully.

'Right, come on then,' he says, getting up.

'Where am I going now?' I say quietly.

The malicious smile spreads further across his face. 'Oh,

you're going on a bit of a journey,' he says. 'But don't worry, you'll be travelling first class all the way.'

I don't question him further but a feeling of dread pools in my guts. I don't like the sound of this at all. He shoves me between the shoulder blades as we go out of the door and I stumble, falling forwards onto my hands and knees. The gravel bites into my palms and I gasp. I hate him. I *hate* him. He squats down on his haunches and looks into my face.

'Oh, clumsy,' he says. 'Did you fall over?'

I look up at him and I can't stop myself. I mouth an obscenity at him, so clearly he couldn't miss it. His grin fades and he stands up. His boot connects with my thigh and I fall onto my side, crying out at the spike of agony. I see him pull his leg back again and I'm too winded to roll away. He's aiming at my head! I think, *Oh God, this is it*, but I hear a shout and the sound of a vehicle drawing up. A soldier comes over – I can see his long, green-clad legs and shiny black boots.

'What's going on here, guard?' says a posh male voice. 'Is this the girl?'

'Yes, sir,' says the guard, crisp and loud. 'She keeps trying to escape, so you'll need to keep an eye on her, sir.'

I creak painfully to my feet, rubbing my thigh where that bastard kicked me.

The other soldier stands very tall and straight. He wears a dark green beret and he regards the guard with a cold expression.

'I don't need you to tell me how to do my job, guard,' he

snaps and I see the other man's face tighten and colour up. 'Maybe if you did yours a little better you would find it easier to hang onto someone half your size.'

A muscle in the guard's cheek twitches, like someone has a fish-hook through it and is tugging on the wire. This image makes me feel a little better. Is this soldier being kind? Is this kindness? I don't even know any more.

'Anyway,' says the soldier, looking at me. There's nothing in his eyes to suggest kindness. Maybe this whole scene is just a bit messy for his tidy barracks. 'It's time to go. Get in.' He gestures to the army truck pulled up beside him which is driven by another soldier. The back has a sort of canvas flap thing and I hesitantly lift it up before climbing into the back. I'm dying to ask questions. Where am I going? What's going to happen next? But my instinct is to keep quiet and be the good little girl. This soldier fella might shoot me without a second thought, despite sticking up for me before.

There are all sorts of ropes and rucksacks in the back here, plus loads of canvas sheets. But I'm only in the back of this truck for a few minutes before it stops abruptly, so that I bang into the side and pain in my bruised thigh shoots down my leg, making me wince.

The canvas flap is yanked out of the way. Another soldier is standing there. He has a gun slung across his front and a different hat from the other guy.

'Come on, miss,' he says. He's got some sort of accent, maybe Scouse.

I go to jump down and he holds out his hand, which I ignore. We're at the side of a main road in a lay-by. Traffic thunders by and I feel the whip of the wind as lorries pass. The soldier says nothing, just stands straight-backed and peering at the oncoming traffic. There's a sound from his radio and he lifts the watch device to his mouth and says something I don't catch into it. I look at the bank behind me and for a second think about trying to run. Then I eye the assault rifle again and know I've got no chance.

About a minute later a large black vehicle approaches. It's covered in thick, armoured panels that look a bit like scales and the window is smoked so I can't see the drivers, up high above the road. They used to call these Black Marias, Mum told me once. Now they're known as CAT boxes, as though the jokey name can take away the fear the sight of them provokes.

One of the doors opens and a woman dressed in a black CATS uniform jumps out. She has short blond hair and pale, icy eyes. She has a volter on her belt, plus a regular gun and a canister of something that's probably crowd gas. I know that stuff will peel your skin off in a second. I swallow. My mouth is so dry. I hope there will be water and something to eat soon.

All my needs are basic ones now. Food. Water.

Survival.

She looks me up and down and nods with her chin at the soldier. He salutes and she nods again. Then she goes to the back of the CAT van and the doors open. A boy – no, a man, but a young one . . . maybe about twenty – falls out onto the lay-by, hard onto his side.

He starts to shout something I can't make out and the woman CAT calmly pulls the gun out from her belt, takes aim, and shoots him. He jerks and his limbs splay. His eyes are open and his forehead has a massive, messy hole. A whistling sound fills my head and for a few moments I can't believe what I've just seen. Some cross between tears and vomit, a cocktail of horror, rises up in my throat and I start to shake hard, all over, as she walks back towards me. Her expression is as blank as if she had just stepped on a fly.

'Deal with that, will you?' she says to the soldier who salutes and taps his booted heels together.

I stare at her with eyes widened by terror at the sickening violence I've just seen.

She looks impassively down at me. She's a good head taller. Her irises are so pale that her pupils are like weird holes in the centre.

'Want to know why I did that?' she says. I don't know how to react. I blink stupidly at her. She carries on speaking and I know I was right not to respond.

'Because he was bitching and whining in the back. Saying he'd changed his mind and that he never signed up to . . .' she pauses and then mimics a whiny male voice, *'no effing boot camp.'* She skewers me with her eyes and then turns back to the soldier.

'Thank you, sergeant,' she says and he snaps a salute again.

She reaches into her belt and pulls out some of the stretchy tape stuff I was tied up with before. Handing it to the soldier, she goes to the back of the CAT van. He kneels down and binds my feet, again giving me just enough space to shuffle-walk, but leaves my wrists free. He doesn't meet my eyes the whole time, even though he's only centimetres away, close enough for me to smell some sort of mint on his breath.

I'm escorted to the back of the CAT van where the female officer stands, doing something to the 3D touch screen on her mobile. Inside I can see there are two rows of seats facing inwards. People are sitting in the seats with bars coming down over their shoulders. It reminds me of a picture I saw once of a rollercoaster at a theme park, where people got dangled upside down in their seats, only held in by restraints like these. I never got to go to a theme park before the bombings closed them all down. I can't imagine a world where people would pay money to frighten the crap out of themselves. It seems to me there are plenty enough ways to do that for free.

Most of the people in the back are looking at the ground, ignoring me in a weird way. Aren't they curious? Then I notice the screen at the far end of the van. I see myself standing there and understand. They saw what happened just now. They're too frightened to catch this woman's eye. Maybe they think they'll be next.

God, what have I got myself into?

Only one person looks out at me, a white girl a bit older

than me who has blond hair twisted into a messy ponytail. She has a sharp face and quick, darting eyes.

I climb into the back of the CAT van and sit in the empty seat nearest to her. The woman jumps neatly up and brings down the arms of the seat over my head. With a sharp click they lock into position. I understand why my hands aren't tied now. The position of the restraints means my arms are wide apart, my hands useless.

'We will stop for a break when we reach Carlisle,' says the woman. But she does a weird thing then. She throws a bottle of water to the blond girl, who nods in thanks. I can't understand it.

And then without another word, she slams the doors closed and I hear a series of clicking sounds, as though several locks are sliding into place.

The engine starts up and the van begins to move. No one speaks.

Trying not to draw attention to myself, I look around at the other people here. There are four others, including the blond girl. A thin boy with a mop of dark hair who looks about my age. I can see his lips moving ever so slightly. Maybe he's praying. A woman in her twenties, with tattoos and short dark hair, has her head tilted away. One of her hands plucks at the material of her skirt over and over again. The last passenger is a smallish black boy about my age who catches my eye and stares at me until I look away.

The blond, sharp-faced girl is looking at me too. I stare

back. I'm not prepared to smile and pretend we're all off on some jolly trip together. I don't know exactly what happened back there, why that man was shot. I close my eyes as the image replays, sickeningly, in my head. I feel a bit sick and force myself to breathe slowly. I'm still desperate for some water. I have no idea how far Carlisle is from here or how long it will be until we get a break.

I've never known time move so slowly. I can't sleep and I don't want to meet anyone's eye. It feels like every second is an hour.

After some time that could be anything from half an hour to half a day we stop. I guess this is Carlisle. I need to pee now, as well as being so thirsty I think I'll go mad. One at a time we're led at gunpoint by a male CAT to some bushes at the side of the road. I try to hide away to pee, embarrassed. I'm given a plastic container of water and I greedily gulp from it, feeling sick because I've drunk too quickly.

Once everyone is back in the van, we move off again. Time seems to slip by more easily now as the miles unfurl beneath the van's wheels. The steady, low hum of the engine lulls me into a sort of nothing state after a while. Every time my mind tries to picture where I'm going I force myself to focus all my energy on a small light in the ceiling opposite. I can't afford to start freaking out here. Seeing what happened to that bloke has made it clear this isn't going to be the easy option.

I try to sleep but I'm too uncomfortable. I want to be able

to move my arms, and my back hurts from the hard seat. I rest my face against the cold plastic of the restraint.

I can't stop myself from doing a quick calculation of my misery, even though I know it will make me feel worse. My face and ear still ache from where Mick hit me. Or was it the guard who did that? It's becoming muddled in my head now. And my thigh hurts like crazy where the guard kicked me. Or was that Mick too? Was he there when the bomb went off, when the farmhouse blew up? It was so loud. And bright. It must have hurt so much when they died, blown to bits, like . . .

Oh, I miss you . . .

I feel a spinning, dropping sensation and then I'm wrenched back to consciousness again.

I open my eyes with a jolt. That girl is looking at me, curiously, again. This time she gives me a weak smile.

'Were you dreaming about someone?' she says. Her voice is high and much posher than I would have imagined. She sounds like she comes from somewhere south, although all the accents down there sound the same to me. 'Is it your boyfriend?'

I feel heat creep up my neck and face. Was I talking in my sleep?

'No,' I murmur. 'I wasn't dreaming about anyone.' I have an instinct not to share anything. I turn my face away, hoping I've closed down the conversation.

But she's not finished yet.

'You look like you've been in the wars,' she says. 'Did one of those bastards hit you?'

I glance around. Everyone else is staring down at the ground or has their eyes shut.

'You should see the other guy,' I mumble and the blond girl gives a weary laugh.

Some time later the engine sounds change and the van slows. We're climbing up a hill and the road is twisty-turny. I close my eyes and try not to feel sick. I keep shaking so I clench my muscles to try to stay still. No one speaks in the van. The blond girl has given up trying to chat to me now and instead sits with her head resting against the arm restraints. Her eyes move under the bluish-white skin of her eyelids and I wonder if she's the one dreaming now.

The van comes to a stop and everyone, to a person, snaps to sit up straight, on high alert.

There's a long pause where nothing happens for ages. Everyone starts to fidget and then the doors are thrown open at the back of the van.

The woman with the cruel face is standing there, her expression blank.

'Well, here we are at last,' she says in a tired voice and then her eyes glitter as her lips twist into something a bit like a smile. 'Welcome to your new home.'

Chapter 9

cloaked

We're herded out the back of the van. The cold darkness seems to wrap itself around me like a dank, heavy coat. The air is different here, wherever we are. I can't work out what it is straight away, it's too strange and new. There's something sharp that reminds me of stuff you'd put in the bath, which tickles my nose.

Then I get it.

It's clean. There's no miasma or filth in the air.

Gradually my eyes accustom themselves to the dim light. Pure, icy panic floods through me then as I decide they have brought us here to kill us.

There's nothing here. The ground seems to swell into hills that might be natural or man-made, I can't tell. There are tall pine trees stretching up into the night sky and in the distance I can make out vast shapes that might be mountains. There's a strange, shimmery effect, though, among the pine trees, and I blink hard, thinking maybe my tired eyes are playing tricks on me.

I glance at the blond girl, who is frowning and looking just as confused as me.

A sharp pain between my shoulder blades makes me jolt forward. The mean female soldier has jabbed me with the butt of the gun.

'Plenty of time for sightseeing tomorrow,' she says. 'It's been a long drive so let's just get inside.'

'Inside . . . where?' says the blond girl, sounding scared for the first time.

The woman mutters something into her phone and there's a buzzing, popping sound as a series of floodlights snap on. There's a huge ugly building ahead on two levels, with blackened long windows. It's a building that definitely wasn't there a minute ago.

'But how . . . What . . . ?' the blond girl gives voice to the confusion I think we're all feeling. Everyone is staring at the woman now with wide eyes.

'It's cloaking technology,' she answers, as though she has said this a million times before and is bored with the whole thing. 'It's what you might call smoke and mirrors. Well, mirrors and light-bending paint, anyway.'

I don't know what she's talking about but a wave of complete exhaustion washes over me then and I think that I don't care what they do to me as long as they let me sleep.

'You'd better get used to it,' says the woman. 'This place is full of surprises.'

We're taken inside the building, which smells the same as the army barracks but with a vague bleachy smell. There are bright lights that make my eyes ache and a few people dressed in normal coats or CATS uniforms walk by, eyeing us as they go.

We're told to line up and an unsmiling man dressed in uniform gives us a small paper cup and tells us to drink. I sniff but it looks like water. The blond girl says, 'I don't want to drink it. I don't know what's in it.'

Without saying a word, the man grabs her arm and has her in a headlock before she can blink. He grabs her jaw and wrenches it open, while she squeals and kicks. He tosses the contents of the cup into her mouth, making her gag and choke but he slams her chin up so her mouth is closed and she swallows.

The girl goes limp, and he lets go of her arm. She doesn't cry, just fixes him with a look of pure hatred.

'It's not going to hurt you,' says the guard. 'But we can force all of you to drink it if we have to.' He pauses. 'Anyone else?'

The others hastily tip the cups into their mouths, never moving their eyes from the guard.

I look at the liquid inside the cup again, hesitating. If they're forcing us to drink something, it can't be good for us, can it? What the hell is it? If I have to be in this weird place, I want to be in control of myself.

I'm not taking it.

I know it's insane. I know I'm only going to get hurt. But all the same I find myself tipping the cup upside down so the liquid splashes onto the white-tiled floor.

The guard jumps back as some of it splashes onto his boots and eyes me with distaste. He sighs deeply and nods to someone behind me. My upper arms are seized by two more guards and they drag me along the floor. I don't even struggle that much. I only wanted to make a point. But now I'm thinking I'm a bloody idiot. We get to a plain white door. They open it and push me inside. It's like a cell, with a narrow cot bed and a toilet in the middle of the room with no lid. It smells rank and my stomach clenches. A woman comes into the room. She has curly brown hair tied back at the nape of her neck, wire-rimmed glasses and a pretty face. She comes over to me and it's only when I feel a sharp scratch that I realise she's plunged a syringe into my arm.

A feeling of deep peace and calm instantly spreads through my chest and belly.

'There now,' she says. 'That wasn't so bad, was it?' I think she says something else but I'm being guided onto the bed now and a delicious feeling of sleepiness is washing over me.

This isn't so bad, I think. *This isn't so . . .*

I'm burrowing down, deep somewhere soft and warm.

I've never felt so safe and warm and sleepy. I'm a little kid again and Mum's singing a song in her husky voice, stroking my hair. I start to laugh because I've never felt as good as this. Am I even *allowed* to feel this good?

There's the smiling woman again and it's her stroking my hair now. She's whispering something to me but I can't really make it out so I just nod, and nod, and then ...

Pain screams through every part of my body and lights blast into my eyes.

People are shouting at me, men with bulging eyes; two women are watching, including the kind one. Her arms are folded.

I'm sweating all over and everything hurts. I don't understand what they want! More pain. I think they're volting me. It hurts so badly. Please stop, please stop, please stop ...

'Enough,' says a quiet voice and a paper cup is held to my lips.

The woman from before has soft brown eyes and pretty eyelashes behind her glasses. She smiles kindly and I drink.

And I'm falling again ...

But just as I'm sinking into the deepest, most comfortable place ever, the lights are on. I'm curled in a ball on the cold, hard ground, too shocked to scream. A pair of cold eyes in a stubbled face looks down at me. I hear a female voice say, 'Go up to level two this time.'

Pain, pain, pain. Everywhere. In my fingers and in my face. My stomach's cramping. Hot pain. I'm being torn apart.

Like when the bomb went off. Everyone dying.

'They died, Kyla?' says a calm voice. 'All of them?'

'Yes,' I whisper, through lips that feel ragged and bloody. 'All of them. All dead. Cal. Jax. Mum. All gone.'

'Are you sure?'

Such a stupid question . . .

Another blast of pain. I don't know where one wave ends and another begins. I'm on a wave of agony and reaching the top. When I get there it will be over and I can die, I can . . .

And the pain stops.

I'm free of this horrible place, running in the fields near the farmhouse. I've got a gorgeous white dress on and my skin hums all over with the knowledge that something wonderful is about to happen. Sunlight sparkles all around and there are wildflowers growing everywhere. And now Cal is here. Alive . . .

He grabs my hand, laughing. He pulls me close and we kiss. It's a good kiss, longer than we had before, that one time. Better. I know that I'm safe at last. *Home.* But then everything gets hot, so hot, and there are flames devouring the flowers and turning everything to blackened stubble. Cal screams out in agony and the skin is blistering all over his face. I reach out to help him and I'm crying too. I think my tears will help him heal and so I touch my wet cheeks and then reach for his face.

There's a booming noise and everything goes white-hot inside my head so I'm blinded for a minute. There's smoke everywhere and when it clears I see horrible things. People torn apart, some of them children. Limbs littering a busy street. Oh God, make it stop . . .Then I recognise someone smiling in the middle of all the wreckage. Who is he? Then I remember. He's the guy from Torch who rescued Cal and Jax from the Facility when it blew up. Tom. That was his name. He's holding a gun in one hand and lifting his finger to his lips to make a shushing gesture with the other. His eyes glint in a weird way. He looks . . . evil. But I turn away from him because someone calls my name. Jax? He's walking in that bouncy way, his long arms with hands in his pockets, and he's whistling. Relief floods through me. He's not dead! I don't have to be alone again. It's all going to be all right.

'Jax!' I yell but Tom is walking towards him and I know he's smiling, but I can't see him. He lifts the gun and shoots Jax through the head. Jax jerks and collapses on the ground. I scream and I try to run to him but I can't because my legs are so heavy.

I'm crying and crying and my head hurts. I'm in darkness now and I try to open my eyes but something is pressing them down. A sliver of light glints and I hear a groaning sound from somewhere. I'm opening my eyes and the light is bright, but then I see faces watching me and feel that my head and shoulders are being held by something tight.

'I think we've probably gone as far as we can for now,' says a woman's voice. I feel myself being sucked somewhere deep and dark.

I'm floating, weightless, like an astronaut drifting through space. I have no body any more . . . no bones and flesh that can break and hurt. I can let everything go. I like it. Time means nothing. The world might be spinning but I'm no part of it now. On and on and . . .

. . . but then I see a pinprick of light and I'm hurtling towards it. I don't want to come back. Please don't make me! But the light becomes a tunnel and then it's inside me and everywhere. Someone is spitting angry questions into my ear, into my brain . . . *'Who, Kyla? Where, Kyla? Why, Kyla? Who? WHO . . . ?'*

And my lips open and words come spewing out like vomit; bitter and sour.

I hear myself say *Cal* and *Jax* several times and every time I say their names, I'm filled with a sadness that's unbearable. It hurts so much. Then I say other names – *Tom, Helen . . .* and my mouth seems to flood with a metallic taste. Tom, Helen, Torch.

'They took away everyone you love, Kyla,' says the voice. 'Torch did this. It's what they do. They kill and hurt.'

Torch, Torch, Torch.

Pain blasts through me again and I hear screaming from somewhere.

Torch, Torch, Torch . . .

And then the pain stops and I'm filled with a feeling that's pure, clean and bright.

Hatred . . .

I hate them . . .

'Why, Kyla?' whispers a voice close to my ear,

encouraging me. 'Why will you kill them? Because they're evil? Because they want to hurt the people you've loved?'

'Yes!' The word comes out as a long hiss of relief. It's like I've been gripping something so tightly that my fingers ache. My whole body has been cramped and in pain. But now I'm letting all that go with one simple word.

'Yes.'

'Who do you hate?'

I shake my head because I suddenly don't want to answer. Pain shoots up my arms.

'Torch,' I whisper, letting it all go again. And the hatred heals all my sore places.

A hand touches my shoulder. 'Good girl. Now, why don't you sleep?'

I don't know what is real and what is inside my head any more. It's so dark it doesn't make any difference if my eyes are open or closed. I feel like a leaf tumbling in a breeze from the tallest tree. When I cry, which I do a lot, my eyes don't make any water. Sometimes I hear whispered voices and I feel water running over my lips. There are sharp pricks into my arms and then I'm floating again, floating . . .

PART II

AREA 6
SCOTTISH HIGHLANDS

From: jsheehy@61.gov.uk
To: aosborne@CATSHQ.gov.uk
Subject: Kyla Baptiste

Dear Alexander,

Having witnessed the full process with this subject I am confident that she is unaware of the whereabouts of Callum Conway. I suggest continuing with training as with genuine recruits. Subject appears to have successfully attained required levels of commitment to work.

We can assess her potential usefulness in the field over the course of the next weeks. I suggest we assign another, more amenable, candidate to monitor behaviour over her time here.

Best regards,

Jennifer Sheehy

CHAPTER 10

stag

I may not 'do' countryside but something about this view really gets to me.

I've run up to my usual spot, behind the camp.

They warn us not to go too far. There's a perimeter fence somewhere nearby. I've been fitted with a tiny, temporary tracker too. But up here I can almost pretend I'm free. I like to stand on this massive hill and just look.

The sky changes so much here. One minute there are bright blue patches and clouds so puffy and perfect they look like the sort in a kid's painting. Then the clouds rumple and thicken, hanging so low you feel like you could put your hand in up to the wrist. I wonder what it would feel like. I know clouds are only water, but I imagine they'd taste like icing sugar if I licked my fingers. Daft. But something about being up here does that to me.

The hills roll out in front of me in a patchwork of purple heather, bright green grass and rich brown earth. Today the sky looks like a churning grey sea that rolls and turns above me.

My skin tingles with the power in the air. I figure a storm's coming. I don't want to get caught in it. But I sort of do, at the same time. It would make me *feel*.

I'm doing OK. Physically, I'm getting stronger and fitter all the time. Even my asthma is better here. But I feel kind of blurry most of the time. Almost like a small part of me is outside, looking down at myself – when I'm getting a tray of food, or learning about the different ways terrorist organisations are put together. But when I get out here, I remember those other bits of myself. I'm me, Kyla, the girl who once liked dancing with her mum in the kitchen. The one who laughed so hard with Jax one day that she peed herself a tiny bit.

The one who kissed a boy, took his picture and then watched him die.

OK, there's plenty of stuff I don't want to feel. Maybe things are better the way they are. Maybe I *am* hard inside now.

I've been at this place they call Area 6 for about two months now. I don't remember much about the time after I first got here. They told me I got sick for a week or so. All I remember is waking up with a throbbing headache in a crisp, clean bed and being told it was time to get up and be useful.

I had some crazy dreams for a while. Dreams so realistic that I started to wonder whether they'd put some kind of chip inside my head, like they did with Cal. And it wasn't just at night. I'd sometimes get these . . . *pictures* when I was awake. I'd be brushing my teeth or something and then out of nowhere I'd get a mental flash of Tom shooting Jax. I don't think that really happened. But I'm not completely sure any more. Things have got muddled up in my mind, like I'm watching screens that have been smashed into tiny fragments and then put back together all wrong.

I try not to think about it too much because it makes me feel weird and a bit dizzy.

I don't know what I expected exactly about this place but I'm definitely not training to be some cool ninja spy. I'm learning to be a snitch. It's not exactly the glamorous job I was hoping for, although they tell us it's important work all the same.

We're known as CATS' Eyes. They want us fit, able to fight. Able to run when we need to. Our job is to watch people and report on them. Like, anyone who's thinking about joining Torch. Anyone who's offering a room or making donations. We'll help to flush them out. But most of all they want us to hate. To hate terrorists, of course, but to hate Torch most of all. And we do. Even hearing that name makes my palms prickle. Surely being a snitch is justified if it stops scum like them? I think about those days at the farmhouse, with Sam being so kind to me, Julia too. That

Nathan guy was sort of grumpy but he still seemed quite decent. Cal didn't know what they were really about. Like me, he'd been fooled into thinking they were the good guys. It makes me want to throw up now.

So I'm getting on with things here. For now, I just want to keep my head down and do what I'm told. I've had enough fighting to last me a lifetime. I'll worry about what comes next when the time comes.

Not that it's an easy ride here. The lessons are a weird mixture of school and army boot camp, with the odd bit of extreme cruelty thrown in to remind us 'this is no holiday'.

For example, let me tell you what happened in one of our Fitness Training sessions.

These lessons take place in a modern building across the courtyard from the main centre, which is all whitewashed walls and sweat smells. There are mats all over the floor and every kind of fancy work-out equipment around the edges of the room.

I'd looked around at the other people in my programme.

I don't exactly have any friends.

The blond girl from the journey here is called Skye and even though we share a bare, cold room (more like a cell) she keeps to herself. There's a lad called Christian, who was the dark-haired, praying one on the journey. He seems OK but spends a lot of time reading and doesn't seem that inclined to hang out. Not that there is anything to do here. We have one very basic recreational room, with a few lumpy chairs they obviously don't want anywhere else. In one corner there's a tiny, old-fashioned television with limited channels that doesn't even do 3D. In the other is the world's oldest PlayStation, which has no 3D either and a controller that looks positively prehistoric. Doesn't work that well but a real loudmouth called Reo and a couple of others spend the whole evening on it.

The trainer is called Lewis, a slim, muscled bloke with short black hair. Not that tall, but he looks fast and strong. Good-looking and knows it.

He told us we'd be working on stealth and said, 'You can be built like a brick shithouse but if you're not capable of moving silently and with grace, then you're basically useless. Like I always say, real life is nothing like the movies. The bad guys don't queue up politely, waiting to be hit.' A low ripple of laughter filled the room then. Jokes are good. We don't get many, let me tell you.

'If you get found out, you're going to be in danger.' His tone was sober now. 'You need to know how to look after yourselves. So . . .'

He went to the back of the room and dragged over a large square container made of thin plastic. A smaller box with slots in it was left at the back of the gym.

'Come and take a scarf and then get into pairs.'

I walked over to the container. Thin scarves in a silky black material were jumbled inside. I pulled one out and twisted it around my hands. It was so light I could hardly feel its silky coolness.

Back at my mat I glanced about to see who I could pair up with. Skye was with Reo. Lucky her. I caught eyes with a woman in her twenties called Zoe and she came over to my mat.

'OK,' shouted Lewis. 'I want one of you to blindfold the other with the scarf. You'll both get a go so it doesn't matter who goes first. Then I want you to take the other scarf and lay it across the other person's shoulder. The person who can see has the job of taking the scarf, unnoticed. If the taker succeeds, place a hand on the blindfolded person's shoulder to alert them they have lost. But . . .' he paused, 'if they catch you, they should immobilise you on the mat. Everyone got it?' There was a low ripple of agreement. 'Right,' said Lewis with a nod. 'Each person take ten turns and then you need to swap. When you've both had a go, sit on the mats to show me you're finished.'

He walked over to a panel on the wall. 'And just in case anyone thinks this is too easy for the blindfolded person, you can't rely on your hearing either.' He wafted his hand at the panel and rock music blasted out of hidden speakers, so ear-splitting and sudden everyone in the room seemed to jump a few centimetres off the ground at once.

I turned to Zoe and we managed to communicate through exaggerated hand movements that I would be blindfolded first. Better to get it out of the way, I thought, hoping she wouldn't take the 'immobilisation' thing too seriously.

She tied the scarf gently around my head, which was a

good start. It felt feather light but still turned the world to a dense blackness. It felt familiar . . . the darkness. It's what I imagine death feels like. I was so distracted by this horrible thought I didn't realise we'd started until I felt the pressure of a hand on my shoulder.

OK, so one to her. The music was starting to make my head ache but I concentrated this time, straining to make out movement behind me. Zoe's hand fell on my shoulder again.

This happened another five times and I was starting to feel humiliated. On the seventh attempt I concentrated on the movement of air around me. Thinking I could feel something, I clutched at thin air. Then I felt the hand on my shoulder again. It was starting to feel like that hand was laughing at me.

Come on, I told myself. *Feel it . . . feel her presence. Smell her . . .*

I tried to pretend there was no deafening music blasting my eardrums. There was just me, and her. The world shrunk around me and that's when I sensed the faintest vibration in the floor beneath my feet. A waft of soap, so slight it was barely there, had me twisting and pushing against the warm, dense body behind me, knocking her to the mat. I couldn't see her but quickly had her on her back, straddling her with my knees. I laughed in delight, relieved I was finally getting it.

On the next two goes, I sensed her each time.

Reaching ten, I snatched the scarf away from my face, blinking in the harsh lights of the gym. Zoe frowned at me and rubbed the back of her head in an exaggerated way. I mouthed, 'Sorry,' and she managed a thin smile. Her turn now.

I blindfolded her and placed the scarf gently on her shoulder.

Looking around the room I noticed everyone was wearing trainers. Almost without thinking, I whipped off my trainers and socks, flexing my toes. It seemed so obvious, I couldn't understand why no one else had thought of it. Moving on the balls of my feet, it was easy to get the scarf two, three, four, five, six, seven, eight, nine times. I was starting to enjoy myself so maybe I got cocky on the tenth attempt. Before I knew what was happening, the world had tipped sideways and my back slammed against the mat. All the air jolted out of me and for a second I couldn't get my breath. I looked up into Zoe's face. She mouthed, 'You OK?' and I nodded as she slid off me.

I was more embarrassed than hurt. Breathing heavily, I wiped the sweat prickling my face with the scarf and sat down on the mat. Almost everyone else had finished, apart from Christian and his partner. Christian turned out to be really good at this too.

We had a knockout contest then and soon it was just Christian and me left.

We exchanged grins and high-fived. This was actually fun!

Lewis regarded us both coolly and then said, 'Kyla and Christian, you've really nailed this task. Well done. Seems you've shown everyone else here up. Come to the front, please.'

I couldn't help feeling chuffed with myself. I wondered

why he wanted us to come up to the front. For a mad moment I wondered if I'd get a prize.

Christian was flushed and looked like he was holding back a grin too, but he avoided my eye. He doesn't give much away, Christian.

'Right,' said Lewis. 'Time for a play-off. We're going to do it a little differently this time. You'll be seated. You don't have to disarm your opponent, just catch them in any way you see fit.'

This time he tied the scarf around my eyes himself and guided me so I was sitting on the mat with my feet poking out in front of me. I felt a bit stupid and exposed. He must have turned on some kind of noise-cancelling thing this time because it went so quiet, the silence seemed to press in on my eardrums. I couldn't hear the other people in the room. All I could make out was my own heartbeat.

I tried to tune in to the vibrations in the room. It was weird, though, because I couldn't pick out anything at all. I started to get a cramp in my leg and moved it, ever so slightly. And at that exact moment, I felt a burning agony in my wrist, making me cry out.

I screamed and moved my arm. And that's when I realised something was attached to my wrist. My other hand closed around something warm, muscular, alive . . .

. . . and scaly.

Scaly?

Wrenching off the blindfold, I cried out again, looking

down at the thick, green snake clamped around my wrist by its jaws. I fell onto my knees and smashed it repeatedly against the ground, over and over. It didn't loosen its grip and then suddenly it went limp and stopped thrashing.

Sobbing, shaking, I wrenched it off my wrist, shuddering at the curved, needle teeth that had been buried into my flesh. Dropping the filthy thing I looked up, eyes blurry with tears. A glass panel had silently divided the room. Horrified faces gazed at me from the other side. Skye had her hands pressed against the glass, her mouth hanging open in horror. I looked to my right and saw another panel separating me from Christian.

He was looking at the ground, shaking as hard as me. A snake lay at his feet, its head caved in. My stomach heaved and I covered my mouth, willing myself not to be sick.

The panels slid up, disappearing soundlessly into the ceiling and walls. Lewis walked over, still with that pleasant smile, like nothing out of the ordinary had just happened.

'The bite is harmless, if a little painful,' he said in a matter-of-fact tone. 'We'll get your wounds tended in a minute but first I want to ask a question of all of you.' He paused. 'What was the point of that exercise?'

No one spoke. Then Skye tentatively raised a hand. Lewis nodded.

'Yes, Skye?'

'Is it, um, that you can't predict where threats are going to come from?'

'Go on,' said Lewis.

'Well, um, because of the exercise that we did just before this, Kyla and Christian were expecting the same sort of thing to happen. I mean, for the threat to be the same.'

Lewis gently clapped. 'Well done,' he said with a smile. 'Top of the class.'

Stomach still churning, I beamed hatred at Lewis with my eyes. It's true that I was expecting someone to creep up on me again, but wasn't there a better way of getting the message across than using a *bloody snake*? I realised now that this was what was in Lewis's mystery box.

I glanced at Christian, who had a trickle of blood running down the side of his hand. It didn't look as bad as my wound, though, which was raining crimson drops onto the floor. It hurt so much, I had to keep checking the snake wasn't still attached to me. I started to shake and had to hug myself to control it.

I run my fingers over the bumpy skin on my hand that still hasn't completely healed, remembering how it felt. I guess the experience was a good reminder that I shouldn't get too relaxed here. I don't think any of us have families out there, judging by stuff I've overheard. No one will miss us if they decide we don't fit in. A mouthy girl called Renna disappeared in the first few weeks. No one wanted to know where she went. Maybe she went to the Facility. I heard some whispers that she ended up in the loch I can see from the top of the hill.

I shiver now as I imagine plunging into that inky

blankness, fighting for breath as water floods my mouth, murky and bitter. I can't swim and the thought of drowning has always terrified me. I think I'd take any number of snakes over that.

All the hairs on the back of my neck seem to ripple then as thunder rumbles in the distance. I've turned to look down at the camp, spread out below. There's not much to see there. The main building looks like something made by a kid with no imagination from grey Lego. There are small windows all across the front in darkened glass. The roof is a mess of satellite-receiver antennae and coiled barbed wire, plus some big square boxes that might be lights. It looks about as welcoming as a smack in the mouth, which is probably the idea. It seems out of place among the swollen purple hills and stormy skies.

A strange creaking sound makes me turn the other way, away from the camp. I gasp. Right there, near the bottom of the hill, is a huge, majestic stag.

It has a tangle of rough brown hair down its front like a shaggy bib. Its antlers are white-tipped spikes, like they've been dipped in paint, and they curl out so high and wide it seems impossible the animal can support its head. We eyeball each other and I feel a weird happiness that fills my eyes with tears. Then it makes a sort of loud huff before dipping down to munch on some grass. I laugh, suddenly filled up with the honour of sharing this space with it, like it has gone, 'Hmph . . . I guess you can stay.' I suddenly want

– no, *need* – to get closer. I can't explain it. Maybe it's because of that muffled, blunted sensation I mentioned before. I don't seem to *feel* so much any more.

And that's a good thing, right?

It's what I wanted . . . to stop thinking about hard things so much.

To stop hurting.

But the stag is all instinct and senses; a series of powerful needs. Kind of opposite to how I've been feeling.

It's *free* . . .

The stag's breath puffs clouds in the cool air. It tears at the grass with its mouth, then slowly chomps away, ignoring me now and totally focused on eating. I'm not important. None of *this* . . . this shit I've been through, is that important.

I've never been the wildlife type. But it feels like the stag is the, I don't know, guardian of all this beauty and I need it to accept me. I would have run a mile from it once. But I'm braver now than I was. I've had to be.

Very slowly, I begin to move forwards. It doesn't move away. It trusts me! I creep a little faster, taking a few more steps, and then . . .

. . . agonising pain rips through me and I'm flat on my back, staring up at the churning sky. Every nerve ending in my body feels like it's on fire and I can't move a single muscle. I lie for a few moments completely still, panting, with tears streaming down my cheeks, before the feeling gradually wears off and I can get shakily to my feet.

I've been volted before. But this was different. This made me feel, just for a second, like I was dying. Sadness clings to me now. The view that had been all colours a minute before is now just grey, wet and depressing. My fingers and toes burn and my limbs weigh heavy and sore.

I guess I've found the perimeter of the camp. I squint ahead of me and can just make out the slightest ripple in the air, now that I'm really looking, like heat reflecting off hot tarmac. You would never know it was here and it's probably only activated by the tracker on me. I glance down at the stag, which chews on, ignoring me. It probably knew exactly how near I could get to it. How stupid to think it was letting me come close. I wrap my arms around myself as a light rain begins to fall and then start to trudge miserably back the way I came.

Like I said, this place is full of nasty surprises.

History of Terrorism, known as HT, is the part of the training that's most like regular school. What I can remember of it, anyway.

I didn't mind school that much when I used to go. Liked mucking around with my mates, anyway. Think I was a bit lippy sometimes. But after Mum got sick I stopped going and although they sent some people round to find me a few times, they didn't bother after a while. Probably presumed I'd died of pig flu too, like Mum and most of the neighbourhood. It was a crazy time, then.

The HT teacher is called Mrs Sheehy and she's older than Mum would be now. Maybe fifty or sixty, I don't know. I'm not good on that. She wears the black clothes they all wear here but hers are a dark skirt and jumper with thick tights and sensible shoes with laces like a nurse would wear.

We sit in a proper classroom with a 3D whiteboard and everything. I quite like pretending I'm a normal schoolgirl, although I don't even know what year I'd be in now.

The lessons are OK and actually quite interesting in places.

We learn loads about the 2010s when suicide bombers were the terrorists of the day. Hard to get your head round in these days of the anonymous little plaster bomb. Why blow yourself up when you can cause destruction and death so easily?

Those plaster bombs are *nasty*. I hear they look exactly like the sticking plasters people used to stick on cuts, which is how they got their name. They're no more than three centimetres square, pale in colour and designed to blend into the background, but packed with enough explosive power to destroy a building. Easy to slip one under a table in a busy coffee shop, or onto the side of a train.

We learn all sorts in this lesson. Truth is, I'm a bit embarrassed by my ignorance about politics and stuff. Like everyone, I know all about the bombing of the Houses of Parliament back in 2017 and how the government was formed out of the parties left over and the army, and renamed the Securitat. That the regular police split into two branches, with CATS having the ultimate authority.

114

I know also that there are lots of different terrorist groups with a million different, confusing names. But Torch is the biggest and the most evil. They're responsible for loads of the bombs that go off in public places. They claim they're all about 'freedom' but I can't see how killing innocent civilians helps them to be free. That's why they have to be flushed out and eliminated, like the scum they are. And that's going to be my job when I get out of here.

It's a couple of weeks after the stag thing. I didn't sleep that well last night. Had weird dreams about Jax. He kept trying to tell me something but his words were all messed up – or foreign or something. I couldn't understand what he was saying. Then I dreamed about kissing Cal. I woke up with damp cheeks.

So I'm not paying too much attention to what Mrs Sheehy is saying in HT, until something snags my attention like a nail.

'We don't know where they got the devices from,' she's saying, 'but a recent operation in the Yorkshire Dales successfully blew up what we think was a major Torch bomb factory.'

Yorkshire Dales? That's where the farmhouse was located. The one they blew up.

Mrs Sheehy points her clicker at the whiteboard and the front of the room fills with an image. Every muscle in my body tenses. The walls seem to pulse and throb around me.

It's the farmhouse. Right after the attack. My heartbeat thuds in my ears and my blood seems to whoosh and pound through my veins. Mrs Sheehy is talking away but I can't untangle the words to make sense. I can only stare at the image in front of me.

If the cameras pan out far enough, you might just make out a girl lying face down in the dust with a cut cheek and a broken heart. Someone speaks.

'Yes, Adam?' says Mrs Sheehy.

A red-haired boy speaks again. 'How can we be sure that it was a bomb factory?'

Mrs Sheehy nods as though she has been expecting this question.

'We received intelligence from an informant within that branch of Torch. And although there are as yet no sensors developed that can detect plaster bombs, the nature of the explosion and traces found by forensic teams in the aftermath confirmed the information.'

I keep my expression completely blank even though my heart is beating so hard it seems to boom in my ears. Clamping my teeth together until my jaw aches, I shove my hands between my shaking knees and stare at the image in front of me, trying to control the violent trembling that threatens to overwhelm my body.

Julia, Sam, Nathan . . . they really were *terrorists*? And then I think of something that makes me gasp and I have to pretend I'm clearing my throat. Would they have tried to turn Cal and me into terrorists too?

This is so terrible. I realise that, for the first time, I'm glad

Cal's dead. Better dead than working for Torch. How could I have been so naive? I want to throw up . . .

I risk flicking my gaze to the sides, to see if anyone has noticed that I'm weirding out. But all eyes are fixed on Mrs Sheehy, who has stopped speaking for a moment. She shakes her head slowly, as though she has the weight of the world on her shoulders. After a heavy sigh, she speaks again. 'Make no mistake,' she says. 'These people had very bad intentions. They would have used those bombs to kill innocent people.'

'Was the mission to destroy the house a success?' asks Skye. It seems like an odd question but I'm too distracted to think about that now.

Mrs Sheehy's face is grim as she clicks at the screen again. 'Only partially,' she says. 'This footage shows the occupants of the house the day before the explosion.'

A new image fills the room. This time the farmhouse is intact and seen through a night-vision infrared 3D camera. You can make out the heat shapes of seven people in various parts of the house. I know that they are Sam, Helen, Tom, Cal's Mum and Dad. Cal . . . and . . .

Oh, shit . . . One of those people is me . . .

I can't stop myself from looking around the room at the others. It feels like my pores will leak the information in some way. I can't keep this inside, it feels too big. Skye is staring right at me. I look away, trying to deny the ferocious heat filling my body.

'Our intelligence told us that there were seven people,' says Mrs Sheehy. 'But we were only able to find DNA from five after the mission.' She pauses. 'So two people got away,' she says crisply.

Then she turns and looks right at me.

'Are you all right, Kyla?' she says, her face softening. 'You're looking a little peaky, my dear.'

I squeeze my hands into fists below the desk, trying to force all the panic there and out of my voice before I speak.

I clear my throat. 'Yes, thanks – I'm fine,' I manage to force out through lips that are numb. 'I was just wondering if it was definitely a bomb factory. It, um, looks like a normal, um, farmhouse.'

Mrs Sheehy gives me a tolerant sort of look. Then the image hanging before us in 3D changes to the moment of the explosion. It's so realistic, everyone jumps back as the black and orange flames curl into the room, out towards us. I hear someone go, 'Woah!' and someone else – Reo, the big meathead – says, 'Burn, baby!'

'The explosion you see here is a lot bigger and the damage more intense than the helicopter fire could have achieved alone. This is basically what happens when you put the equivalent of a match to twenty boxes of plaster bombs.' She pauses, her expression grave. 'This is the kind of people we are fighting. And each one of you . . .' She looks around, meeting eyes with everyone individually. They seem to linger on mine even longer. '. . . will come out of here knowing how to do it. How to stop the rot before it spreads.'

Afterwards, I pretend I have a headache and go to lie on my bed for a while. The walls are white-painted stone with a small window too high up to be any use. I lie on my stomach with my face pressed into the pillow, wishing I could scream.

So first of all I hear that the people who looked after me were harbouring bombs in that house. I know they were Torch and I know that Torch are evil, but it's only now I can admit that a tiny part of me hoped Sam and Helen and the people who helped Cal and me were different. Seems I was wrong. I was so stupid and trusting. I should have known better than to expect any decency from Torch people.

But the thing I can't take in is that two people somehow escaped that blast.

One was me.

Who was the other?

Could it have been Cal? And if it was . . . will I ever see him again?

CHAPTER 11

banana

I'm in the rec room watching some soap with half my brain. Trying not to think about the future. It takes me a while to work out what it is I'm feeling, and then I realise.

I'm bored. I miss having a laugh. Everyone is so serious here. *No one* could crack me up like Jax, though. He didn't always mean to, which was the funniest thing of all. It was one of the reasons he was so easy to love. A pang goes through me and I draw myself into a ball, my feet tucked underneath.

Think about something else, I tell myself.

Skye comes into the room then and plonks down next to me on one of the big cushions.

'Watching that?' she says, tipping her head towards the telly.

'No, not really,' I say.

She taps at the remote until she finds a music station. 'It's my birthday today,' she says suddenly.

'Oh, hey,' I say. 'Happy birthday.' I think about my last one, when I was at Craydale Farm. I picture Ariella's face, with that upturned little nose and her bright eyes. I wonder whether she misses me and what they told her. She's probably used to people coming and going. I mentally shrug away the thoughts. I'm not going *there*, either.

'How old?' I say, sitting up straighter and turning to Skye.

She does a huge yawn and stretch so that the sleeve of her top rides up a bit. I see silvery scars on her arm and look quickly back at the television.

Even though we share a room, I feel like I don't know her at all. She stares at me sometimes and then smiles but other times she seems like a robot. Like nothing is going on inside.

'Sweet sixteen,' she says and then bursts into a manic sort of laugh. 'Pretty big deal, eh? They used to have special parties for the sixteenth. My mother had one where her parents hired a pink stretch limo and she took sixteen friends to a luxury spa.'

Hearing her mention a mother is a surprise. Everyone has a mother, even if they don't have them any more. But Skye could have hatched out of an egg for all I know about her.

I don't know what to say, so I just smile gormlessly. She's staring at the floor now, chewing on a nail and looking like the saddest person ever. It makes me want to do something. But partly just because I'm restless and twitchy tonight.

121

Energy seems to be building in all my limbs.

'Wait here,' I say. She looks up, half frowning, half smiling.

'Wait for what?'

'Just wait, OK?'

I race down to the canteen. When it's closed for the night you can still get fruit and bottles of water. The lights are low as I arrive but when I step into the vast room brightness floods the space. I know there are motion sensors everywhere. For a second I freeze, wondering if I'm going to get into trouble for wandering about at night. I don't for a moment think I'm not being watched. But when nothing happens a few seconds later, I walk over to the counters, heart thumping loudly in my chest.

I choose a bunch of the ripest looking bananas, a plastic fork (we're not trusted with proper cutlery, despite the stuff they teach us here) and a paper bowl.

Feeling a bit giddy inside, I hare back to where Skye is waiting. She's sprawled out across the cushion with her legs hanging over one side, patting the rhythm to a song with her fingers.

She frowns when she sees what I'm holding.

I come over and hunker down over the table.

'I got excited for a minute there. Thought it might be cake,' she says in a dry voice.

I mash up the bananas in the bowl, pounding them with the fork until they're a brown mess. Feeling doubtful about my idea now, I plaster on a smile anyway. What am I doing? I have no idea. Maybe I just want to have a laugh for once. I was always doing daft stuff with Jax. I think my mouth has forgotten how to make giggle shapes now.

'No cake,' I say. 'And we can't go to a spa. But we can bring the spa here!'

'What?' Her eyes twinkle a little, her lips curling into a small smile. It's not a look I've seen on Skye before. It suits her. 'In what way is a bowl of stinky banana a *spa*?'

I put on Mum's Jamaican accent. 'This is some of nature's goodness right here, girl! Ain't no need to be spending money on no face packs.'

Skye gives a throaty giggle. 'Forget it,' she says. 'There is no way I am putting that,' she points a disdainful finger at the bowl and then at her face, '*there*.'

The devil is in me now. I put my fingers into the bowl and scoop out a big dollop of the gloopy banana and smear it across my cheeks.

Skye watches me the whole time, starting to grin.

'That's a good look on you. Still not doing it, though.'

I can feel that devil inside, even stronger now urging me on.

'Oh yeah?' I take another scoop of the banana and go to put it on my face but at the last moment I take aim and splodge it straight at hers. She gives an outraged squeak and leaps to her feet. For a split second I think I've made a mistake. Her eyes have gone weird, like all the light has gone out of them. I actually think she's going to punch me. Then her mouth twitches again and she calmly takes the bowl from my hand, spoons some of the mixture out of it and slaps it, a tiny bit too hard, across my cheek.

I rub it in and then lick my fingers. 'It's not bad. But I've just remembered it's supposed to have a whole load of other stuff in it.'

'Like what?' says Skye and helps herself to another handful. This time she dabs at her forehead. She's playing along now. I'm a bit more relieved than I'd like to admit. She scared me for a minute there. But then I suppose it *is* a bit dumb to throw smushed banana at someone when you don't really know them and we are all being trained to fight.

We sit down, all relaxed now, and dab the mixture around our cheeks, trying (and failing) not to get any in our hair.

'Yogurt, for starters,' I say. 'Bit of avocado used to find its way in there too. Although I don't recommend guacamole. Chilli burns like hell.'

Skye regards me and licks a bit of banana from the side of her mouth.

'Are we having fun yet?' she says.

'Not sure,' I reply. 'I'll get back to you once I've got this disgusting banana off my face.'

For some reason this lights the touchpaper and we're off, giggling helplessly – so hard, I fall forwards and get congealed banana on the sofa. It feels so good to laugh. Skye keeps snorting and that sets me off even more. It's a chain reaction; every time she's starting to get control of herself, my hysteria goes up a notch and then so does hers.

After a while we sit up and wipe our eyes. We both look a right mess. Her eyes are shining with laughter tears and her hair is all over the place. Mine has banana in it. (Not something I would recommend for curly hair.)

There are only a few people around across the room. I see Reo watching us, then he saunters over. He stinks of the Lynx fragrance capsules he swallows all the time. I'm sure you're only supposed to take one of those things a day, but I reckon he swallows the tabs and still douses himself in the old-school body spray. It never seems to mask the stink of sweaty man-boy he gives off anyway.

'What are you two up to then?' he says. 'Bit of girl-on-girl action on the cards? What the hell is that on your faces?' He gives a sort of whooping laugh. 'Trust me, ladies, you're already ugly enough. Don't go making things even harder for yourselves.'

Skye sits up straight and stares at him. That dead look is back in her eyes.

'Get lost, Reo,' she says. All the laughter has evaporated into the air.

'Free country,' he says and flumps down heavily onto the sofa next to me. I nearly fall into him. I suddenly want this stuff off my face more than anything in the world but I don't want to give him the satisfaction of knowing he's spoiled our fun.

I sit there, unsure about what to do next. I'm half looking to Skye for a cue. 'Maybe I'll have a go,' says Reo and puts his fingers into the bowl.

Then he leans towards Skye. I can't believe his cheek. Does he think she will actually let him touch her? She moves fast. It seems like half a second later she's squatting over him and holding the plastic fork right by his eyes. I can see the dark, sticky mess coating the plastic, but the tines are sharp enough to damage him. I don't have any doubt in my mind that she would do it. The knowledge is just there, complete, in my head, as I'm guessing it is in hers too.

Reo smiles and then spits in her face, shocking her so that she flinches and drops her guard. He grabs her wrist and twists her sideways off him and onto the floor. She catches her face against the table as she falls and cries out in pain. I jump to my feet to help her, as Reo gives a nasty laugh. He gets up easily.

'You're a complete jerk, Reo, do you know that?' I say through gritted teeth, reaching down to help Skye get up. But she brushes my hand away.

Christian comes into the room then and stops abruptly, his eyes widening. It must be a very weird scene. There's me with half-dried gunk all over my face, Skye is slowly getting up from the floor with the same, plus a small cut on her cheek, and although Reo is smirking, he still looks a bit red and nervous. I think Christian is going to say something, but he just backs straight out of the room again.

Reo stalks off, still chuckling in a really infuriating way.

'Right, well, I'll leave you two bitches to carry on playing your little games,' he says. I do a rude hand gesture at his back and then look at Skye again.

'You OK?' I say. Skye's hands are trembling as she touches the sore place on her cheek. She nods.

'He's such an idiot,' I say.

'Yes,' she says, in a strange, distracted sort of voice. 'He really is.'

'Come on,' I say, 'let's go wash this stuff off and see how gorgeous we are underneath.'

My joke falls a bit flat. She meets my eyes, not smiling, then nods. 'Yeah, let's do that.' She seems to be somewhere else. So much for our girly bonding session. A sour feeling of disappointment spreads in my stomach. I was enjoying myself – for a little while then I felt like a normal teenager. Should have known it wouldn't last.

I make my way back to the bathroom and wash my face. Then I remember I've left my hoodie in the TV room so decide to nip back to get it.

No one is in there now because we're close to the ten o'clock curfew. There are only a few minutes left so I pick up the hoodie and go to hurry back to my room. I feel something crackle in the pocket. That's weird, I'm sure there was nothing there before. I reach in and find a small piece of paper. On one side there are printed words: *Inside the Terrorist Mind: A Psychological Primer by J. Martin Smith*. It looks like the title page of a book that someone has ripped out. I turn it over, curiosity flickering inside. At first I think there is nothing there but then I make out very faint words, written lightly in pencil. I have to hold the paper close to my eyes to be able to read them.

Don't trust her

I look up and around, but can only see one of the patrolling guards, doing a curfew check. He gives me the evil eye and I quickly explain that I'm on my way back to my room.

When I get back, Skye is in bed, facing away from me. I go into the bathroom and rip the paper into tiny pieces before flushing it down the toilet. I have to flush twice before the last flakes of paper swirl away. The note must have been referring to her. I wonder who left it?

I climb into bed and switch off the light, turning to face the wall. I don't think sleep is in a hurry to come tonight. A million unwanted thoughts crowd into my head.

Like, what is going to happen to me after I leave here? No one has told me exactly how long I'll be in training. I'm starting to get a bit comfortable.

OK, it might not be ideal. I get locked in at night and the guard's expression just now was a reminder that this is 'no holiday camp' as we keep being told. I didn't really choose to be here at all.

But I've got food and a bed. Once I'd given up Zander's dubious protection I had none of those things. I'm relatively safe here.

Aren't I?

'Kyla?' Skye's voice takes me by surprise. Her voice is husky but she doesn't sound sleepy at all. I turn back the other way to face her. There are floodlights outside on the courtyard and even though our window is tiny, there is always a silvery glow seeping into the room.

'Yeah?'

Her eyes gleam in the dim light. 'That was nice, what you did.'

'What?' I murmur. 'Throwing banana-mush at your face?'

She gives a low laugh. 'You know what I mean.' She yawns. 'You're all right.'

A pleased flush floods my face.

'Happy birthday, Skye. Sweet dreams.'

'Yeah, and you, babe. Night.'

I turn over onto my other side again, aware that a heavy sleepiness is starting to come at last. I told myself before that I wouldn't get close to anyone again. And I won't. But it can't hurt to let my guard down a little, can it? She seems OK, Skye. Bit weird and damaged, but who isn't round here? And that's just the staff . . .

And then I think about that note. *Don't trust her.*

I don't need anyone's advice. I've looked after myself this long, haven't I?

I reckon I can handle Skye.

CHAPTER 12

connections

We're in History of Terrorism a few days later. Reo has been giving me these little smirky looks every time I see him. He tries to do it to Skye too. But she blanks him in a way I can't help but admire. I swear he could come up and wave in her face and she'd still manage to ignore him. It's quite impressive.

Mrs Sheehy looks pissed off today. She blinks hard a few times and doesn't smile as people come into the room as she usually would. Everyone picks up on the atmosphere and falls into silence. She takes a very obvious breath in as though gathering her strength and then lifts up a book, holding it as though it might burst into flames at any moment.

'I'm a tolerant woman,' she says in a cold voice I've never heard from her before. 'I know that some of you have had difficult lives, but that is no *excuse* . . .' At the word 'excuse' she takes hold of the book with the other hand and waves it at us, 'for vandalism of books!'

'What d'you mean, Mrs Sheehy?' says Skye in a small voice.

'I mean, Skye, that someone has ripped a page out of this book!'

Curious now, I peer at the cover but I know what the title will be even before my brain registers the words.

Inside the Terrorist Mind: A Psychological Primer by J. Martin Smith.

Mrs Sheehy continues to complain about the damage to the book but I tune her out, slowly allowing my eyes to track the room. Only one person is looking back at me. Christian. He doesn't blink or look away. Understanding passes between us as surely as if he'd spoken. It was him who left the note for me. I slowly turn back to face the front.

What's his problem with Skye? He barely talks to anyone here so why has he taken against her in particular? I spend the rest of the lesson only half listening, chewing this over.

At the end I try to catch his eye again but he hurries out of the room.

Later, I go for a run, trying to clear my head. I drive myself hard, even though it's raining steadily. My feet pound the wet earth and splatter mud up my legs. My chest aches with exertion and the only sounds are the *huff-huff* of my breathing and pattering raindrops.

When I get to my usual spot I stand and look at the view,

which is only partly visible through the mist. Today it looks like a watercolour painting that someone has smudged and smeared; green merges into purple, which blends into brown.

Finding my breath again, I think about cracking up with Skye before. And a wave of longing to see Jax comes at me like a punch, so powerful I groan and wrap my arms around my middle. I stand there for ages, absorbing the pain but holding back the tears that are trying to come. I keep thinking I'm over this. That I'm numb inside. But maybe some losses never stop feeling like fresh wounds. Is Cal dead? Despite everything, I almost hope he is. He's a *good* person. He would have been corrupted by Torch if he'd lived.

As for me, I don't know exactly what kind of person I've become.

These thoughts cling to me, as damp and heavy as the air outside, as I make my way into the canteen area later.

I glance around, noticing there are quite a few of the older CAT recruits here tonight. We don't see them that often. They never speak to us and we never speak to them. Occasionally they will give us a curious look and I've definitely been eyed up a couple of times by some of the younger men, but I always give them what Mum used to call The Look. Some of them laugh and some of them squirm a bit.

The noise level is high tonight, with conversation and the clinking of plates and cups. A gust of laughter comes from a corner of the room where a really hard-looking bunch of men, all bullet heads and no necks, are leaning into the centre of the table and reading something on a tablet.

I weave between the tables and chairs, noticing Christian sitting alone. It's an opportunity to speak to him about the note. Then I see Skye's watching me two tables over from him and decide now isn't the time.

'You look like you're somewhere else,' says Skye kindly as I sit down opposite her.

I shrug and take a mouthful of the shepherd's pie I've absent-mindedly heaped onto my plate. It's a bit cold and the mashed potato feels sodden and claggy in my mouth. I put down my fork and drink some water.

'I know that look,' says Skye in a low voice. 'That's a boy look.'

I'm so surprised at her half-accurate guess – even if she can have no way of understanding the background – that I almost splutter the water across the table. She giggles and gathers her fine blond hair at the back of her neck, whisking it up into a scrunchie. The sleeve of her hoodie slips back and I notice the scarring again. But I quickly avert my eyes from her arms and back to her face. I don't know if I was quick enough. I don't want to make her feel self-conscious.

'Look, babe,' she says in a much softer voice. 'I've been meaning to tell you something.'

'What?' I say. Nerves flutter in my stomach.

Skye looks around. 'It's just that you sometimes talk in your sleep.'

'God.' I feel my face go tight and hot. 'Do I really?' I'm cringing inside. I used to do this when I was really little. Mum told me. But I didn't think I'd done it for years.

'Er, what sort of things do I say?'

Skye chews her lip. 'Well, sometimes you say a name I can't make out . . . sounds like Mal? Hal?'

I look down at the table. 'Cal,' I say softly.

'And he's "the boy" is he?' Skye does air speech-marks with her fingers. I nod.

'But Kyla . . .' Her voice has gone even more serious so another feeling of unease ripples through me.

'What?'

She leans in close and conspiratorial. 'Was he . . . you know, in a certain organisation?' She mouths 'Torch' at me and I hastily look around to make sure no one else has noticed. But everyone just carries on around us, eating and talking.

'Why?'

She brushes her long pale hair back off her shoulders. 'It's just that you've said the name a few times too.'

The desire to share what I'm thinking with her is suddenly so powerful, it's like something tugging inside my head.

I give a deep sigh.

'Not really,' I say in a low voice. 'They helped him – us – for a while, yeah, but he didn't know what he was getting himself into.'

Skye frowns and then tips her head to the side, questioningly.

And before I can stop myself, words pour out of me, fast and free like the little pile of sugar that must have spilled from a container on the table in front of us. I tell her about Cal and how he came into my life at Zander's. I tell her about how he gave me his antibiotics when I was so poorly from pneumonia and how really, he might have saved my life. I miss out loads, of course. I don't tell her anything about him being in the Facility, or the Revealer Chip, or what happened with Jax and the explosion. I don't specifically tell her about the farmhouse. But I do tell her about spending time with Torch and that he died. I don't mention that he might be alive somewhere. Skye doesn't say anything much, just makes sympathetic noises in the right places. Her eyes are a bit distant again. I wonder if she's thinking about her own past and hope she'll share something with me. But when my voice trails off, she just carries on eating her salad, taking small, bird-like bites of lettuce, her eyes cast down.

Finally she speaks. 'It sounds really rough,' she says, still not meeting my eye. Then she drops her voice to almost a whisper. 'Best not to mention his connections too much around here, though, eh?'

I nod and then try to force down a bit more of the shepherd's pie. I've just trusted Skye when I had been specifically warned not to. What's wrong with me?

And it's not just that which is worrying me. I nearly lost it earlier, in the HT class. All the painful emotions from my old life came flooding back. If I'm honest with myself, that blurry, blunted sensation has been wearing off for a little while now. It's like I've been enclosed in bubble wrap but now I'm starting to emerge and *feel* again.

From nowhere, a memory of Julia hugging me after Jax died swerves into my mind, making me suck my breath in sharply. She was a *terrorist*! I need to hate her. I need to hate them all . . .

It used to feel like the easiest thing in the world.

But something is shifting inside.

And that frightens me.

CHAPTER 13

a fear of heights

I try to get on with things for the next few days. Working hard on my lessons and running to my limits so all I can do is collapse at the end of the day. It stops me from thinking too much.

I've convinced myself that what happened between Skye and Reo is forgotten. Even though he quietly mutters things to her when he passes, she always swans past him with her head held in a dignified way. I'm really impressed at her resolve. He makes me want to growl and hiss.

We've been learning to abseil in the gym. I've always loved to climb, ever since I was a little girl. Like I said, I've got a head for heights.

So when we're told by Lewis that we're moving from the gym to one of the rock faces in the grounds, I'm glad of the change of scene and to be outside for once.

There's a little sunshine today. I tip my head back and enjoy its kiss as we troop outside, past the outbuildings and towards the main gates. Lewis and another instructor get our group of eight to pile into a jeep with some climbing gear. Before we left, our trackers were disabled (temporarily, we're told) because we need to get beyond the perimeter field.

The jeep twists along a narrow road for a few minutes until a mountain swells into view. Sheep dot the scrubby grass in woolly blobs. When we stop and pile out near them, they check us out with their freaky eyes before hurrying away. Someone makes a convincing sheep noise and everyone laughs, even Lewis.

Reo, though, is the only person not laughing. His eyes look glassy and he keeps swiping a hand across his brow and swallowing. What? Is the big bully actually scared of heights? I lean over and whisper in Skye's ear.

'Check out Bigmouth over there. Looks a bit green, doesn't he?'

Skye follows my gaze and grins back at me, her eyes shining. I know she's enjoying seeing him squirm.

We climb a little way until we can curl around onto an outcrop of rock. It's about fifteen metres up. Lewis explains that this is going to be the starting point for everyone to abseil back down the mountain. There is a bag of harnesses in the back of the jeep and Skye volunteers to get it and hand each one out. She seems to take ages, and Lewis eventually shouts at her to get a move on before we all freeze our butts off.

Finally we're all stepping into our harnesses.

I'm with Christian, who is looking a bit pale and anxious too. I give him a reassuring smile and double check his harness after he checks mine, as we've learned to do.

'Come on,' I say, 'we'll go together. It's easy-peasy.' We step backwards over the edge of the rock face at the same time.

It's much more slippery than in the gym. The rock has slimy places and I lose my footing about halfway down, swinging into the rock and scraping my knee painfully. My pride is hurt more badly, though. I get to the ground a little after Christian to catcalls and cheers.

Skye and Reo are next but they don't come down together. I wonder whether Skye got the opportunity to hiss something about how high it is to Reo. I can just imagine her doing it and I can't help but grin at the thought. He wouldn't hesitate to wind someone else up, that's for sure.

Skye glides down the rock easily; gracefully. Her cheeks are flushed bright red and she is breathing heavily as she reaches the ground. I wonder whether she found that more scary than she was prepared to let on. Typical of her to keep everything inside.

Reo comes next. He's such a dick, he hasn't bothered to do his helmet up properly, but has left the straps loose around his chin. Lewis doesn't say anything. This isn't school. The attitude here is, you get told safety stuff once. If you get hurt, it's too bad. It's also your problem, and only your problem.

Reo stares down at the ground, his face set and grim. Then he swears viciously and begins to edge down the rock face.

And then he slips.

There's a collective gasp and someone mutters, '*Shit*.'

Reo's feet scrabble at the rock but somehow he flips backwards so he's almost horizontal to the cliff face.

'It's OK, don't panic,' yells Lewis, cupping his hands around his mouth to protect his words from the harsh wind that has started to whip up now. It flings rain into our faces, hard and sharp as gravel. 'Just bring your legs down a little bit and place your feet flat against the stone,' he says. 'They need to be lower than you've got them, but not too low. Come on, Reo, you've done it lots of times back in the —'

Reo drops, fast and heavy, hitting the ground with a dull thud. His helmet lies a metre or so away, uselessly.

Lewis runs over and everyone crowds around. There's a sort of poisonous excitement in the air. Reo breathes in shallow gulps, his eyes stare straight up and are clouded with fear. His leg is at a weird angle and one arm is bent underneath him.

'Don't move, Reo!' says Lewis as he fumbles for his phone. He gets up to try to find a signal but he isn't hurrying. He doesn't seem too worried. Is it because he thinks Reo is going to be OK? Or because he doesn't care either way? We all say encouraging things to him, like, 'Hang in there, Reo!' and, 'It's gonna be OK!' Everyone except Skye, who stands a little further back from the group. She has that weird look she gets sometimes. Like she's zoned out, her eyes glassy.

'Oh God,' says someone. 'What's happening to him?'

Reo's body starts to jerk like someone is pulling him from side to side. Pink froth bubbles at his lips and his eyes are open but staring at nothing. Lewis flings his phone aside and runs over before crouching down and heaving Reo over onto his side.

Reo stops jerking and goes absolutely, frighteningly still.

Lewis places his fingers at Reo's throat and swears. He turns him onto his back and starts to perform chest compressions, then breathes into his mouth, pinching Reo's nose.

But he only does it three or four times and then stops.

'Shouldn't you carry on a bit longer?' I cry. I've seen them do it on telly for *ages*.

Lewis gets nimbly to his feet and sighs.

'No point,' he says. 'He's had it.'

I suck in my breath and glance around at everyone else. No one is meeting anyone else's eyes.

'Wait here while I try again to get a signal,' says Lewis and he runs the long way around to the outcrop where we started.

I don't know what I'm doing. But I drop to my knees anyway and squat over Reo's broad body. I clench my hands into the same double fist shape I saw Lewis make and start to pump at Reo's chest. One, two, three . . .

I stop and attempt mouth-to-mouth, cringing a bit at the intimacy of being so close to him. But it feels hopeless and after a few minutes I get back to my feet. Everyone is looking at me with a mixture of horror and open curiosity. Only Christian gives me a weak sort of smile.

No one speaks. I clutch my elbows and hug myself against the cruel wind blustering around the outcrop. That's when I catch Skye looking at me. The expression on her face is so strange that at first I can't work it out.

Then I suck in my breath as it all starts to make sense.

Can it be *disappointment* that I'm seeing? Like I've failed a test of some kind by a small act of humanity towards Reo. She actually shakes her head then and I know that I'm right.

It's so callous. Surely she isn't happy he fell?

And then other horrible thoughts roll together like a line of pool balls dropping into a pocket.

Skye was the person who gave out the harnesses.

Could she have meddled with Reo's on purpose? I start to shiver now and look over at Skye again. She's watching me, her lips slightly curled up as though she's amused by all this. I look away, disgusted by her. A throbbing sound from above makes me look up. A helicopter gets lower and lower, bigger and bigger, until it lands close by, scattering us all as the wind brutally whips up leaves and twigs. Two people I've never seen before, dressed in the blue clothes of the medical wing, stroll over in no particular hurry. They lift Reo and dump him on the stretcher in a way that makes me wince. Surely he's more than just a slab of meat now? He might have been a bit of a git, but he probably had a family once, somewhere. People who loved him. The tears surprise me when they cloud and sting my eyes. I quickly blink them away. What's happened to tough Kyla who doesn't care? I didn't even like Reo.

I suppose I'm just wondering whether anyone would care if I had been the one who fell down a mountain and cracked my head open.

After a few more minutes I watch the helicopter beat a path back into the sky, its blades whumping a rhythm that seems to rumble inside my bones.

Lewis sharply tells us to follow him back to the jeep. His face is pale; his jaw set.

I start to walk after him, my head lowered.

'What's with the lifesaving bollocks?' says a dry, low voice beside me. Skye has caught up. Her hands are in her pockets and her head is high, despite the slapping wind and rain. 'Anyone would think you were mates or something. Come on, Kyla, he was a total jerk!'

I stop walking and turn to her. She coolly meets my eye. 'Skye,' I whisper. 'Did you . . .' I swallow, as her frown deepens. 'Did you have anything to do with what happened there?'

She stares so blankly for a second I think I've made a terrible mistake. I'm about a second away from trying to stuff the words back in my mouth and mumble a pathetic apology when a tiny smile creases the sides of Skye's mouth.

'I don't know what you mean,' she says in a strange, expressionless voice. 'It was just an accident.' And then she smiles again. Her pupils are dilated and her eyes seem all blackness. For a second she looks . . . wicked. It's the only way I can describe it. Then she leans in and whispers in my ear, so close I feel hot breath on my cheek, 'Wasn't it, Kyla?'

Lewis stomps past me, jerking my attention away from her.

'Get a move on, you lot,' he says. 'This has really mucked up the afternoon.' Then he mumbles, bitterly, 'It'll be effing paperwork all the way for the rest of the day.'

Shocked, I say, 'Will there be a funeral or anything?' and Lewis actually laughs. I gape at his retreating back. Doesn't he care at all that a boy just died?

Inside the truck I look around at the rest of the group. Everyone is a bit quiet, but by the time we're back a few conversations have sprung up. Even Christian looks quite relaxed as he yawns and watches the scenery go by. I stare at him so hard he turns and meets my eye. I make a questioning face but he looks away, pointedly.

What's wrong with everyone here?

Is this how I'm supposed to be? Isn't there some middle ground between not allowing myself to get hurt, and being totally dead inside?

We're told we can have the afternoon off. But I don't think it's because they care about anyone being upset. It's probably so they can sort out the paperwork caused by Reo's inconvenient death.

I don't want to speak to Skye so I avoid our room and instead veg out in front of an old movie in the rec room. But I'm not really taking it in. I keep hearing the sound of Reo thumping to the ground and picturing the useless helmet lying nearby. I'm not going to grass Skye up. And anyway, maybe they wouldn't care that much. But I'm not hanging out with her any more. I'm starting to wonder what kind of people this place turns out.

And whether I want to be one of them . . .

Christian wanders in when I'm lost in thought and at first I don't notice him at all.

He sits on a chair opposite me and crunches loudly into an apple. I look over at him with a start.

We eye each other for a few moments. I suddenly feel angry; agitated.

'So that's it, then,' I say sharply. 'Someone dies and they just disappear? There's no more mention of them? Done,' I swipe my hands together, 'and dusted, eh?'

Christian regards the half-eaten apple and then throws it neatly into the waste-paper bin on the other side of the room. He looks around and then comes to sit a bit closer, looking at me intently.

'A word of advice, Kyla,' he says. 'You're not meant to care about this stuff. You're going to attract the wrong sort of attention if you make a big deal out of this Reo thing.'

'Oh, and you're such a hard man,' I say. Almost spit, really.

His brow creases and his lips tighten. He sits back and looks away. And I realise something, way later than I maybe should have done.

Christian likes me. *Likes me* likes me. I look down. I can't even think about stuff like that. He's not bad-looking. But everyone in this place feels like damaged goods and I've got enough of my own worries to be dealing with. And anyway, I'm never letting anyone else in. I've promised myself that.

'Why'd you warn me before?' I say now, trying to shrug off the slight embarrassment my realisation has brought. He looks up, a defiant expression on his face now. 'About Skye,' I go on. 'What do you know about her?'

Christian looks around again and then speaks in a low, conspiratorial voice. 'OK, so something happened on the journey here,' he says.

I gnaw a fingernail as anxiety flutters in my stomach.

'You remember that boy they shot?' he continues.

I make a face. 'How could I forget that?' I say.

'Yeah, well, he hadn't stopped talking on the way,' says Christian. 'About how he was only coming here to get out of prison and that he was going to escape as soon as he got the chance. He came out with a whole thing about how Torch were going to bring down the regime and free everyone.' Christian swallows and looks down at his hands. 'It was all talk. He was just trying to show off.' He looks up again. 'Anyway, when we stopped to collect you, Skye asked to speak to the commanding officer in private. They shot him right afterwards. And *Skye* was given something to drink and allowed to sit more comfortably. It was obviously her reward.'

Chills run down my arms. I reach for my hoodie. Pulling it on, I zip it up and wrap my arms around my legs.

I don't know what to say. Would Skye really do something like that? But I already know the answer to this question. I think about her expression earlier. She looked disgusted when I tried to help Reo. Like I'd let her down in some way.

'You know earlier . . .' I start to say and then Skye is walking into the room, drinking a bottle of water, her hair loose around her face. Her eyes are bright. Too bright. As though she's glowing from the inside for all the wrong reasons.

'What are you two talking about?' she says. Christian sits up and away from me. I square my shoulders and meet her eyes.

'Not much,' I say.

'I'd better be getting off to bed,' says Christian hurriedly. He gets up and gives a really fake yawn. 'Night.' And any slight ideas about whether I could be with him in different circumstances melts away.

It's every person for themselves here. Fine by me.

I mumble, 'Goodnight,' back and watch Skye as she slumps down on the sofa next to me. She starts to watch the film, a mocking look on her face. 'God, did they really dress like that once?' she says. 'Check out the mullet on that guy. And is he wearing *leg warmers*?'

I ignore her. I actually can't stand to be near her any more.

She let someone die for a bottle of water.

She killed someone else just because she didn't like them. She's toxic.

And actually, I am a little afraid of her now, even though I don't want to admit it. I uncurl and get to my feet. 'I'm off to bed,' I say stiffly.

'OK,' she says in a careful sort of voice, eyeing me. Her lips are a thin, tight line. As I walk away, she calls my name.

I turn round to look at her.

'You have sweet dreams, OK?' she says.

Feeling a bit flustered, I turn away and carry on walking.

In the bathroom I brush my teeth, looking at myself in the mirror as my mind whirrs. My eyes look big and fearful.

Keep out of her way, Kyla, I tell myself. *Just keep out of her way.*

But a few minutes later, as I curl up under the cheap, thin duvet that never properly warms me, I wonder how I'm going to do that when I have to share a room with her.

I don't know how much longer we're supposed to be here. And it's with a jolt of horror that I remember how I opened up to her before. Could she try to use it against me now?

CHAPTER 14

three minutes

I pretend to be asleep when she comes in and then creep out of bed before Skye in the morning. I can't keep this up but it'll have to do for now.

We're learning about plaster bombs in Explosives Training. The trainer is a woman called Mrs Harris, who has a face that doesn't seem to move much.

Plaster bombs are creepy. The only way to disable them is to fully immerse them in liquid. But chucking a glass of water at them isn't enough. They have to be properly soaked.

We're halfway through the lesson when Harris says, 'Right, I think it's time for you to see what you've learned. Come on, everyone.'

We follow Harris across the courtyard towards the building where all the gyms are. Instead of going in the usual direction, we're led down several flights of stairs into a gloomy basement and towards some big, glass double doors where an armed guard sits, looking bored. Harris speaks to him and he lets us through. We're facing a corridor with a series of plain white doors.

'One room each,' says Harris, unlocking the one in front, which happens to be right by me. I step into a small, white room. There is a table in front of me and cupboards around the walls. A potted plant is on a shelf high up. Fake, I think, although they're so realistic now it's hard to tell.

It has been set up to look like an office up in here. There's even a half-full glass coffee pot and some cups laid out on a tray, plus a small sink with a dishcloth hanging over the tap.

I stand there, not knowing what to do, when a crackle from some speaker in the ceiling reminds me that I'm being watched.

'Now Kyla,' says the voice of someone I don't recognise. 'Your job is to identify the location of the explosive device and then disable it. Do you understand?'

'Yep.' Well, this isn't going to be that hard. There's very clearly a sink there. I'll bung it under the tap. It's not as though it's going to be a real bomb. Maybe they just want to check whether we've been listening properly.

A digital clock display floats up out of nowhere in the middle of the room. It says 03:00.

'You have three minutes to complete the task,' says the voice, 'beginning now.'

02.59.

'OK,' I murmur, bending down to have a look under the table. It's hard to see all the nooks and crannies under there so I feel around with my hand, trying to find the telltale feel of soft, papery plastic we've handled in other lessons.

Nothing there. I check the chair next, then stand on it and open the cupboards, one by one.

I'm balancing a bit precariously and feeling at the top shelf when a loud *BOOM* from somewhere outside makes the walls shudder. I'm knocked from the chair. I crash painfully onto the hard, tiled floor, twisting my ankle.

'What was that?' I yell. I'm thinking earthquakes. There have been a few small ones around the UK in the last ten years. There was one in Cumbria that killed a couple of people when I was living at Zander's. I wince and rub my ankle, which is already starting to swell.

'That was one of the students failing the test,' says the voice calmly. 'These are live bombs, Kyla. Please resume the task.'

LIVE? What kind of sadists are these people? Could they really do this? Then I remember the snake incident.

They're monsters. But I have no time to waste now. No time to think about anything else but finding that bomb.

I start to look in the same places again, my fingers slipping with sweat as I bang open cupboard doors and frantically feel about inside every surface.

Think, think!

01:15.

I clamber onto the chair and then hoist myself onto the

151

sink so I can reach the plant. I pat around the pot and then feel something on one of the huge glossy leaves.

Turning it over quickly, I see the small, grey patch stuck to it. It looks so harmless. But we've been told a plaster bomb just three centimetres square could destroy a two-storey building. I rip off the leaf (real) and climb down again, accidentally putting weight on my hurt ankle. I whimper in pain. But a busted ankle is the very least of my worries as I run painfully to the sink, glancing at the projected clock as I go.

00:25.

God, the bloody sadistic bastards . . . I wonder whose bomb exploded and how hurt they are.

All these thoughts are running through my head as I carefully lie the leaf holding the small, deadly device in the sink. Will the impact of the water detonate it before the moisture can penetrate the plastic? Taking the leaf out again I lay it on the side and fumble for the plug, stuffing it into the hole with fingers that are almost useless because they are trembling so much.

I twist the tap as hard as I can.

And nothing happens.

There's no gush of water.

The sink remains completely dry. Whimpering with terror now, my whole body shaking violently and my breath coming in short, squeezed gasps, I look round the room.

00:10.

Oh God, it's going to go off – what am I going to do?

00:08.

Then I spy the coffee pot containing the cold coffee. I pick up the leaf again, trying not to squeeze it or shake it and force myself to move carefully across the room to where the pot sits.

00:05.

I pull at the lid, but it's wedged down firmly.

'I hate you, you bastards!' I scream. 'I hate you!'

00:02.

I bang the pot down on the table and it's enough to dislodge the lid. I'm plunging the leaf into cold coffee as the clock switches to 00:00.

Sliding onto the floor, panting, I try to catch my breath. And then I start to cry, wishing I could stop, as relief chugs through me.

'Well done, Kyla,' says the cool voice. 'If you could please leave the room now. You will find that the door is open.'

I'm too washed out and hollow to move.

'Kyla, please vacate the room now.'

I slowly get to my feet and only just manage to resist lifting a finger to the cameras to show these people what I think of them.

Emerging from the room, I see Skye and Zoe and Christian, all looking dazed like me. Christian has a huge gash on his forehead and his eyes are wide and frightened-looking.

I quickly look around to see who is missing . . . who failed the test.

'It's a simulation,' says Skye. She's a little pale but looks in better shape than the rest of us. 'The rooms are rigged to move and shake as though someone has set off the bomb. We were all safe the whole time.'

'How do you know?' I ask. 'It's not like they care about us, is it?' I regret it immediately. Words can be dangerous when Skye is around. I think about the boy who was shot.

'It's obvious,' she says, in a patronising way. 'They're not going to let their valuable *building* get destroyed every time they do a training exercise are they?'

She's right. Of course she's right. Anger boils up at them for letting us believe we were about to die.

'You've got to admit it was effective,' she says. 'There had to be something at stake or it wouldn't have meant anything, would it?'

'What's wrong with you?' I hiss, and her eyes widen.

'What's wrong with me?'

'Do you think this is all some sort of game?'

Skye takes a step back. 'Kyla, I'm sure you can't mean that,' she says loudly. 'You'd really rather have gone to prison than be *here*?'

'What?' I say. 'That's not what I . . .'

It's only then that I notice Harris has come out of one of the doors and is watching us with interest. Skye turns and flicks her hair away from her neck.

I think it's only me who sees the small smile on her lips.

What the hell is she up to? Why did she say that?

INTERNAL EMAIL: STRICTLY CONFIDENTIAL
From: jsheehy@61.gov.uk
To: aosborne@CATSHQ.gov.uk
Subject: Re: Kyla Baptiste

Dear Alexander,

Following our earlier discussions, I have some further information. In the light of the subject's previous Torch connections, Skye Rafferty was assigned to keep an eye on her behaviour and commitment. I had thought the subject was making good progress and am therefore disappointed to learn that she has been quietly stirring up trouble and saying she is not fully accepting our work here. Ms Rafferty suggested that Baptiste may actually still harbour Torch sympathies, but confirms she is unaware of Conway's location.

I am unwilling to throw away the clear potential this girl has so suggest that she undergoes a second commitment-training period. I appreciate this isn't often attempted and that there are risks attached. But I think in the circumstances it is warranted. If she subsequently remains mentally intact, she could be a useful recruit in the field. And there has to be a chance that she might ultimately lead us to the boy.

I await your quick response in this matter.

Regards,

Jennifer Sheehy

From: aosborne@CATSHQ.gov.uk
To: jsheehy@61.gov.uk
Subject: Re: Kyla Baptiste

Dear Jennifer,

I agree with your stated course of action. But rather than merely repeating the procedure, I think that in this instance we should move up to level three and employ all techniques available (full sensory deprivation, use of pharmaceutical enhancers and increased image bombardment, etc). We know the effects typically only last six months at most, and usually wear off quite suddenly, but she does appear to be a particularly stubborn candidate. I will respect your opinion as to potential further use.

Having lost two candidates already in this cycle, though, please try to ensure the girl survives the treatment, as questions may be asked about use of resources.

Warm wishes,

Alexander

CHAPTER 15

nothing to worry about, Kyla

I can't sleep.

Every time I'm close to dropping off I see the numbers of that clock projection going down, down, down . . .The bedclothes are damp with sweat. All I can do is toss and turn and wait for morning to come.

It feels like days pass before pale grey light begins to bleed through the tiny window above Skye's bed.

Her hair is spilled in pale strands across her pillow. I still can't believe what she said to me last night.

I'd gone out for a run after the horrible Explosives practical, hoping I could get my head together. The damp, clean air felt good after being in that claustrophobic room and I came back feeling more clear-headed, but ready to find out what Skye thought she was doing outside the room, when she made it sound as though I had been slagging off the course.

But she managed to avoid me for the whole afternoon and most of the evening, too. I'd showered, eaten, watched telly and caught up on a bit of written work Mrs Sheehy wanted without seeing her at all. I didn't know where she'd been when she finally came into the room, but her cheeks were flushed and she wouldn't meet my eye.

As she went to get her towel for a shower, I jumped to my feet and blocked the entrance to the bathroom. Her eyes widened and then went cold and flat again.

'What was that about earlier?' I said.

'Don't know what you're talking about,' she said and tried to push past me. I shouldn't have done this, but I was raw and upset about the events of the day. My head felt like it would pop with the pressure. My arm shot out and slammed her backwards against the bathroom door. I pinned her there with both hands. I'm taller than her, so I forced her to look up into my face.

'Get your filthy black hands off me,' she said in a voice that was one low hiss of hatred.

Shock hurtled through me and my arms fell to my sides. Skye quickly pushed her way into the bathroom and slammed the door. I sat down on the edge of my bed, shaking all over. She's never said anything before to make me think she was racist. I couldn't have felt more surprised and upset if she had spat in my face. What was that *about*?

When my heartbeat eventually slowed down I thought about the things she'd done to people. Maybe I was lucky that a nasty insult was the worst she'd thrown at me.

But I knew I couldn't share a room any more. I decided there and then that I would ask if I could be moved in the morning. I'd say a breakdown in our friendship was making it hard to study or something. I didn't want to have to share air space with someone like her. Skye was bad, through and through, and I had to stay out of her way.

I must have dozed because the next thing I know, the morning alarm cuts viciously into a confused dream about running through bombed-out houses in Sheffield. My mouth feels dry and foul and the lack of sleep makes the light outside burn my aching eyes, which don't seem to fit the sockets properly any more.

Skye gets up and practically runs out of the room, without speaking at all. She doesn't even bother to wash or brush her teeth, just pulls on clothes and hurries past me, a flush spreading across her cheeks as she deliberately avoids meeting my gaze.

I'm slow this morning. Tired and feeling emotionally wrung out. I'm just trying to braid my hair in an attempt to stop it from looking like a bird's nest, when there is a gentle knock at the door.

'Just a minute!' I call and walk over to open it.

'Oh . . .'

Outside there are two guards and a woman who at first I can't place. Then I remember that I saw her the day we arrived.

She has dark brown eyes behind her glasses and a pretty smile.

'What's going on?' I say, nervously eyeing the guards, who stand with impassive expressions.

Dread floods my stomach like cold water. I get a flash of something I can't hold on to in my mind. Something bad. I step back, suddenly overcome with the need to get away from these people.

'Don't even think about it,' she says, still smiling. I jolt because it's like she has read my thoughts. 'You need to come with us for a little intensive therapy. It's for your own good. And the good of the camp.'

'What do you mean, intensive therapy?' I can't keep the wobble out of my voice. 'Is this what you did to me before? Is it why I can't remember a whole week?'

I'm taking backwards steps the whole time, as if I could just melt through the walls and disappear. Get out of here. I have such a bad feeling now. I don't want to be here any more. I don't want to do this. Maybe they'll let me go?

The woman gives a tight smile. 'We don't always know what is best for us, Kyla. There's really no need to panic. No one is going to hurt you.'

She does a weird slapping motion and I feel a sharp pain. There's a tinkling sound as something falls to the floor. The plastic shell of a mini syringe lies at my feet. I look down at my hand. The outline of the tiny, dissolvable needle is already starting to fade as its contents seep into my bloodstream.

'I'm not . . . Why are you . . . ? I don't . . .' I mumble, my tongue thick and hard to manoeuvre, before the world does a sickening three-sixty spin and I feel myself sliding towards the stone floor.

Lights.

Pain.

Too many voices, shouting.

Pictures.

Bad pictures. Make them stop. Need some water. Why won't anyone help?

More pictures. People being hurt. Whose fault? WHOSE?

Someone's fault.

I hate them.

Hatred is pure and good. It will heal me. Just make the pain stop. Help me . . . ? Someone? Anyone?

A dark room. Then lights that are too bright. Voices jabbing at me like needles.

Over and over.

So tired and hungry. Please let me die now?

Please.

I fall into a dark place. There's no time now. This is the end.

But then I'm soaring through the sky to the mountain. Shadows wash the green with swathes of darkness. Everything speeded up, like a film running too fast.

Sunlight breaks through and sparkles on the lake in the distance, diamond bright. Clouds race above me, scuttling across the surface of the sky like living things. They make me dizzy so I look away and concentrate on the purple heather and the clean, fresh air in my nose, filling my lungs with purity.

I know they're not real, but it doesn't matter. I can stay here for ever, I hope. A noise startles me and I look down to see the stag below me, close by. It looks up directly into my eyes, which fill with tears. I suddenly love the stag. So much that it hurts. Glancing down at my feet, I see a gun with a thin, black barrel.

Do it, Kyla . . . says a voice. It's inside me and outside too.

'No,' I say, 'I can't. I don't want to.' But even as I'm saying this I'm reaching down for the gun. I can't stop myself. I grit my teeth, trying with everything I have to resist the force inside me that's making me pick up the weapon.

The stag doesn't move. Doesn't sense the danger.

It's too pure to be kept alive. It has to die.

'Sorry,' I whisper, and I raise the gun. There's an ear-splitting crack. The stag totters and falls sideways to the ground. Its eyes are milky now, a messy wound spreading red between them.

And I feel . . . nothing at all.

PART III

LONDON,
FIVE MONTHS LATER

CHAPTER 16

kizzy jones

I stare up at the dirty, smeared window above me. Raindrops slide and chase each other down the brownish glass. I look around the room at the other sleepers, lumpy shapes that snore, twitch and give the odd groan. Smells creep up my nose. Unwashed bodies, tobacco and weed, farts, feet and breath. Disgusting here.

But I'm hoping it won't be for too much longer. The endgame is in sight.

I sit up and a headache sears across my forehead. I get them a lot these days. I wince and rub my temples and the pain passes.

'Hi,' the husky voice comes from next to me and I glance down at Adem, his dark eyes sleepy and soft. I feel a flash of something tender and quickly dismiss it. But I smile and snuggle down next to him anyway, feeling his warm arm coming round to hold me close. Soon his breathing settles back into sleep and I wait a bit before carefully slipping free and gliding soundlessly to my feet.

There are too many people crowded into this room, either in tatty sleeping bags or with worn rugs and old coats covering them. I step carefully over them and make my way to the bathroom where I wash my face and try to tidy my hair a little. I get my toothbrush from its hiding place behind the loose tile and brush the staleness away from my mouth, looking at my reflection in the brown-spotted mirror. You have to hide everything in this place or it becomes public property.

My skin is a sort of greyish colour at the moment. I know it's because I've been living in these slums for a couple of weeks, never going near a fresh vegetable and absorbing the dampness and dirt of the bare brick walls. My chest is tight and I can hear the wheeze starting to come back so, hiding the toothbrush again, I find the breather stick and soon feel the cool relief as my lungs relax.

When I was at the camp, I didn't have any problems with my asthma. It was the air there, I think. Pure and clean. Here in London it's even worse than it was in Sheffield but if I was to wear the expensive miasma mask folded to nothing in my bag, it would give the game away. That I'm not really homeless Kizzy, on the run from her abusive stepdad, but Kyla, CATS' Eye. The girl who, if things go as expected today, will never have to see any of these people again. For a second, a wave of doubt washes over me and I picture Adem's expression earlier. Full of trust. I close my eyes and breathe deeply, looking inside myself to the place I know will ground me and show me the right way. I hear that lilting, soft voice saying, 'You are fighting evil, Kyla. It's war. You are light in the dark place.'

Dark place . . .

I was in a very dark place for a while at the camp. I only remember snatches. It feels a bit unreal now, like a film I once saw. Being alone inside the white room flashes into my head. I remember crying. Pain and then relief as the pain stopped. The room filling with images of terrorist victims. A young boy crying next to smoking rubble. An old woman being shot in the head. And worse. Sounds come back to me sometimes too, weird noises like cats fighting and high-pitched singing. But the weirdest one of all, which surely can't be real, is hearing the theme tune from the kids' programme *Here's Gomez!* over and over and over again.

Here's Gomez! Here's Gomez! He's got r-attitude!

Here's Gomez! Here's Gomez! He's got r-attitude!

I shudder and pull my thin top over my fists as I remember, wrapping my arms around my middle. Then there was the soft voice again. The voice I came to love. I slept for a long time then and when I woke, Mrs Sheehy's face was the first one that I saw, kindly smiling down and smoothing my hair away from my cheek.

I asked her why I was there and she said I'd been ill but now I was safe. I couldn't remember what happened just before I was in the hospital wing. Everything felt sort of hazy. Still does. But like I always say, I'm no hero. I'm just trying to stay alive. I reckon what I don't know can't hurt me. I've got this far, haven't I? When I left the hospital wing, Christian was strange with me. Didn't speak to me much any more. But luckily Skye soon helped me get back on my feet.

All I wanted was to work hard, to make up for missing time I should have spent learning. Learning how to defeat our enemies and keep the world safe.

To help destroy Torch.

As always, a shiver of disgust goes through me at that name. And that makes the image of Adem's smiling face dissolve in my mind. OK, so he's cute and funny, with a quick mind that flits from one topic to another so fast I can't keep up. And he might think he's out to make the world better, but he's got it so, so wrong. Because he's one of them.

It's not my job to help him understand that. It's only my job to help him and his kind get caught.

I just need the name of the person he's reporting to and I can make the call.

A loud rap on the door makes me jump. The breather stick clatters onto the dirty, sticky floor.

'Hurry up in there, yeah?'

'Sorry!' I call out, hurriedly putting the stick back behind the tile and securing it with the glue-tac balls that keep it in place.

I open the door. Magda grins at me, revealing her

missing tooth at the front. She's forty-something and her head is a mass of twisty dreadlocks, threaded with jewel-coloured scarves. Her eyes twinkle even though they're red-rimmed from partying the night before.

'Have you finished with the Jacuzzi?' she says. It's a running joke between us, that really we live in a millionaire's palace instead of a filthy squat, where damp and mould coat the walls and you have to watch where you tread or you could stand on a week-old pizza, a full ashtray or a sleeping person.

'Yeah,' I bat back, 'I'm going to call for breakfast now and take it on the veranda. Hoping the buff butler brings it this morning.'

'Well, watch out for the pigeon shit out there, eh?' says Magda, collapsing into a cackle that quickly turns into a wet, smoker's cough.

I smile and step past her, disgust roiling inside.

Do I feel guilty about what's going to happen later? It's a question I ask myself from time to time. I asked myself with the first job I did when I came to London, working in a nursery school and then reporting on the woman, Stevie, who ran it. It was hard leaving the little kids behind afterwards, and not easy watching Stevie being dragged away with a blackened eye and an arm that hung in a weird way. But it's getting easier every time I do a job. And I haven't killed anyone . . . not directly. That seems important. I just flush them out and what happens next isn't my business or concern.

It's what I do now. And it's for a good cause. I know I used to feel things too much. Inside I was a mass of softness. I'm not soft inside any more. I'm strong and I'm hard. And I only bruise on the outside.

Adem's up now and when the bathroom is free, he goes for a shower. Cold, which is the only sort of shower on offer here at the crumbling old building that is Hoxton Mansions, London. He grins at me, distractedly, as he emerges from the bathroom with black hair seal-wet against his head and a manky towel under one arm.

I return his smile and then regard his retreating back. Something's definitely up. I can feel it. There's an electricity in the air; a sense of expectation. But why?

Adem has been weird for the last couple of days, checking his phone too much and laughing too loud at my jokes. He practically crackles with nerves. He's almost blue-lit, like he's been volted. But he hasn't shared anything with me, despite lots of dropped hints and teasing kisses on my part. By the afternoon I've decided I have to up the stakes. I've had enough of this job. I want a bath, some clean clothes. Some decent food.

I go and sit in the bay window on the top staircase. It looks out over the street . . . well, it would, if you could see through the smeared, cracked glass that lets wind whistle through it like a ghostly cry.

If he can't find me straight away, he'll come looking. He's so lovesick, he can't bear to be parted from me for a minute.

I make myself cry for authenticity and rub my eyes hard. I can do this. Sometimes I wonder what it would be like if I was an actress in movies, rather than this. But there's no point in thinking that way.

Soon enough I hear the distinctive creak of the broken stair. I bury my face in my arms, drawing my knees in close so I'm a ball of misery.

'Kiz?' His voice is gentle and I feel a warm hand on my arm. 'What is it? What's wrong?'

I look up at him blearily, seeing the concern on his face. 'It's nothing,' I say in a thick, snotty voice.

He sits next to me on the big window ledge. 'It's not nothing, is it. Tell me?'

I stare downwards, letting a single tear roll down my cheek. He gently brushes it away with a finger.

'It's just . . . today. It's the anniversary.'

'Of what, Kiz?'

I give a huge, trembly sigh. 'Of when they took my dad away.'

'Who did?' Adem's voice is so quiet it's just breath.

I look deep into his eyes and whisper, 'CATS.' And then, 'I *hate* them.'

There's a long pause. For a second I wonder if I've played this wrong. What if he ended up reporting *me*? I almost laugh at that thought and have to keep control over my face muscles, keeping my mouth turned down at the corners and my eyes gleaming with sadness.

'What happened?' he says at last, his voice low and deep.

'They said he was a terrorist,' I sniffle. 'That he belonged to all sorts of banned organisations. That he was organising meetings in our neighbourhood. But he was a good person!' I blurt, louder. 'He ran the football team, he organised all the social things like barbecues and picnics. He didn't have a bad bone in his body!' I let a sob escape and then continue, as though the words have to pop out painfully, one at a time. 'But they came early one morning and beat him in front of us all. Dragged him away. No one saw him again. And Mum,' I take a big, shaky breath, 'she never got over it. She took some pills . . .'

Wow, I'm laying it on thick but I'm doing such a good job I can practically see the scene before my eyes.

The pearly, dawn light, the shouts puncturing the quiet of the sleeping street as the innocent dad is dragged away.

He sounds much nicer than my real dad, the loser Mum told me about. The one who left her, pregnant, and went off with the army, never to come back from the war. It's my fantasy so I'm going for a handsome but cuddly sort of dad, with a bald head and an easy smile. Heck, I'm actually feeling sad for the poor, made-up sod myself now . . .

Adem pulls me into a fierce hug. I rest my face against his chest and smell the cheap soap powder he uses to wash his clothes by hand. He rests his cheek against my head and speaks in a voice so low, I have to strain to make out what he's saying.

'Look, I shouldn't tell you this and you have to forget I ever did, but I agree with you. Plenty of others agree with you. Plenty.'

I pull away and meet his eyes.

'I know,' I say. 'But I wish I could do something, you know? Fight back in some way?' I swallow. 'For my dad.' God, I'm really trowelling this on. Adem looks at me for a long time then. Again, I wonder if I've blown it, and then he leans over and gently kisses me on the lips.

'I'm not making any promises, but maybe you can,' he says then, his eyes as serious as I have ever seen them.

I pretend to look confused. 'But how? Even talking about joining Torch is against the law.'

I whisper the word 'Torch' and Adem shifts uneasily.

'I know I can trust you, Kiz,' he says.

You really can't, I think.

'Someone is coming here today,' he continues. 'Someone important. They're going to lay low for a while in the basement. No one in the house is meant to know about it. But I'm telling you because maybe this person might be able to find a way for you to do what you want . . . fight back.'

I grab him in mock excitement and plant a kiss on his mouth.

'Who?' I say. 'Who is it?'

He seems to hesitate again and then leans over and whispers a name into my ear. It's the name of a senior member of Torch, someone the CATS have been after for years.

I swallow back the gasp but let the excitement shine through my eyes.

'I won't tell a soul,' I murmur, and lean in for another traitor's kiss.

Like I said, it's what I do now. I might feel a little bad later. Or I might not. Mostly, I just want a bath.

CHAPTER 17

reveal, enhance

L ater, I lie back, inhaling the smell of expensive bath oil. Steam rises around me and I stare upwards at pure white tiles, so different from the cracked, rotten moulding that covered the ceiling at Hoxton Mansions. I wave a hand vaguely at the wall and, as News 24/7 appears on the hidden screen, I wave again to set it to 2D. It's a bit weird having 3D people in the room when you're in the bath.

The ticker is running along the bottom of the screen saying *Senior terror suspect killed in bomb blast* and I sit up so fast that water sloshes over the sides of the tub onto the heated, marble floor. I grip the edge of the bath and stare at the screen as the newsreader talks.

'*It's believed that the man, Jack Richardson, was one of the most senior operatives in the illegal organisation Torch. We have a live statement from East London now.'*

The screen fills with the image of four men sitting at a table for a press conference. They all wear CATS uniforms.

The camera flashes to a face I know. A face I last saw in the back of a car in Yorkshire after Mick attacked me and I fought back. The man who ultimately put me in this room, right now. The ticker reads: *Alexander Cameron, Chief Commanding Officer of the Counterinsurgency and Anti-Terrorist Squad.*

'This afternoon we took part in an operation to capture a senior member of the terror organisation, Torch. After attempting to arrest Mr Richardson by peaceful means, our officers had no alternative but to take decisive action when residents of the house he was hiding in opened fire. In order to protect innocent civilians in the neighbourhood, we launched an attack on the building. The bodies of Richardson and four other people, also believed to be Torch members, were later found.'

I hit the panel on the side of the bath and tap the fan unit in the ceiling into action so that seconds later, the air is clear.

I wonder if Adem was one of those four bodies and sigh deeply before getting out of the bath, sloshing more water over the sides. Grabbing one of the thick, fluffy towels, I wrap it round me. I love these towels. They're filled with crystals that mean they stay dry on the surface and are always just the right temperature.

I slowly dress, pulling on the silk tracksuit bottoms that are so soft they whisper when I walk and feel almost weightless, and a light cotton T-shirt. I'm glad I can wear good clothes again, glad I can lie in that luxurious bathroom for as long as I want, knowing I will come out to a fridge stuffed with food and anything I want to drink.

I pull my hair back and brush in the special oil I've just discovered, which makes it fall in silky waves around my face. I look at my reflection and see a girl with eyes that are too old for her face. I've already lived too many lives. Seen too much. Sometimes I get so tired . . . And then I'm *crying*. Great big, wet, heaving sobs that start like someone flicked a switch. What the hell?

This keeps happening and I have no idea why. It's like the weird headaches that have suddenly started coming. It's like things are . . . coming apart inside me.

I stop crying as abruptly as I started and feel cleansed now, as I always do. Washed on the inside. I put a little make-up on under my eyes and some lip gloss, and heave a sigh. The luxurious bath I was dreaming about for the past three weeks didn't feel as good as it was meant to.

Padding barefoot down the corridor, I hear television noises coming from the sitting room. It's about the size of a whole floor of the flats where I grew up in Sheffield, and looks out over the Thames. It's like being sealed inside an airtight container up here. I suddenly miss the noises of London and even the dirt, a little, as I walk into the vast room. The floorboards are golden and shining, warm underfoot. My feet seem to whisper over them.

Huge, soft sofas in buttery yellow are arranged around the main screen. One of the walls is covered in big paintings that I think are ugly, but they double up as sound boards for the meetings that sometimes happen here.

As I come into the room, I catch sight of a different story on the news.

It's a woman who has somehow got herself up onto the scaffolding around the new Big Ben building. I cringe when I see her face. Her eyeballs are exposed and the skin is rippled and sagging around her jaw, her cheeks drooping and puckered like molten wax.

Disgusting.

They call them Melters. These are the people who, in protest at all the CCTV surveillance, use a chemical synthesised from liquid plastic to disfigure their faces. And then they promptly get arrested, of course. So pointless. What do they think they will achieve?

But there is another reason I always look away from Melters.

It happened when I hadn't been in London that long.

I was walking along the Strand one day, in a hurry, when I noticed someone all scrunched in a doorway like a bunch of rags. It was a boy, about my age, I think, but it was hard to tell because when he looked up, his face was horribly disfigured, shining like rumpled, pale plastic from inside his blue hood. The sight sickened me to my stomach and I looked away quickly. But something bothered me all afternoon that I couldn't identify.

It was only later, as I was drifting off to sleep that I realised there was something familiar in the boy's eyes. I think that boy might have been Christian . . .

What could have happened to make him *do* that? I couldn't stand thinking about it.

I must have made a sound at this thought because a blond head pops up now from one of the sofas.

Phoenix is a few years older than me, from what I can tell, which makes him a veteran. I haven't come across any CATS' Eyes who are older than early twenties. I reckon it's because they go off into other jobs after doing their stint. I asked about it once, but no one seemed all that sure. I don't like to think about the alternative. I guess what we do can be dangerous. People must bear grudges. And the bad guys don't always get caught, do they?

'Hey,' says Phoenix, uncurling his long body from the sofa. I nod a greeting and then go to get a drink and some fruit from the fridge.

Phoenix switches channels, settling on a documentary about flood defences.

I arrange pieces of watermelon, grapes and apple on a plate, enjoying the overlapping, bright colours. When I've been working, I feel as though I want to eat only healthy stuff. It's partly because of the rubbish I have to eat on a job. But I think it also helps me to feel clean again, on the inside. Doesn't make a lot of sense.

I sit facing the wide window, looking out at the river and the skyline. Sunlight glitters on the Thames and on Westminster, beyond. There's the original Big Ben, which is kind of cute, and the grand, golden building where they used to make the laws. The river sparkles as boats chug along it. Clean water you could swim in.

It's all pretend. Suddenly sick of the false image, I murmur, 'Reveal.' The smart glass reverts from the enhanced mode to a normal window.

Now there is only a building site where the Houses of Parliament stood. The new building is costing millions, I hear, but there have been all sorts of hold-ups. All you can see is a web-like mass of scaffolding.

I stare at the churning water of the Thames as I suck on a sweet, juicy sliver of watermelon. The sky is one sweeping bruise of black and grey, the rain never-ending. I heard that the county of Suffolk is practically all bogland these days. Wherever Suffolk is.

Someone told me the other day that the Thames was filthy in the past, then it got majorly cleaned up. People used to catch fish in it in the early 2000s. Hard to imagine now as the slimy, almost green water bobs with refuse . . . and worse. Sometimes you see a dead dog floating along with the shopping trolleys and the plastic crap.

Suddenly sickened by the sight of the water, I murmur, 'Enhance,' and the windows shift back to the pretty view. As soon as I step outside, I'll see the real thing again but it's good to be able to pretend sometimes.

'I need to shift my ass,' says Phoenix, interrupting my thoughts. He gets up and stretches luxuriously. 'Places to be.'

I don't ask where. Just as he wouldn't ask me what I've been doing. We come and go to this flat when we need it, to log our reports and rest between jobs. Realising I still need to log mine, I sigh deeply, staring down at my half-eaten plate of fruit.

I suddenly have an urge to be moving, despite the rain outside. There's an amazing gym downstairs but I'm not one for gyms. I think I'll go for a walk. Try to clear my head a bit.

I use my breather stick and then grab my miasma mask to be on the safe side. When I could first afford one, I used to get annoyed about the fact that they only match white skin. But I don't care about that so much now. There doesn't seem to be much point in getting angry about stuff I can't change.

Sometimes I think I'm a bit dead inside. But if I am, what's with the weird crying?

I'm thinking about all this as I take the glass lift down to the ground floor and make my way past the security guard. He's called Bob and he always gives me a smile but I've seen what hangs from his belt, weapon-wise. He's not there for decoration.

I pull my miasma mask on. This is the most expensive sort you can get and you don't really feel it once it's on. You do still look like a freak with a snout. But at least you're anonymous.

The rain has stopped for once and the slick pavements gleam and reflect splashes of street lights. I pull my hood up and hunker my hands down into my pockets. I look a bit like a boy when I'm dressed like this. And I can handle myself these days. I have a thin-bladed knife that snaps into the treads of my trainers, hidden. I've never had to use it. Yet. I walk past the homeless shelters under the overhanging lip of the Southbank Centre. Someone told me that kids used to skateboard there. I glance over, trying to imagine what it would have looked like then. There are layers of graffiti, some so old it has faded into the brick as though it is part of it, with newer, more vivid designs over the top. Hard to imagine people using this place for fun.

Now it's somewhere homeless families live. No single people allowed. CAT teams regularly sweep in and make sure there are no drugs, alcohol or any other 'banned substances'. I think at first they tried to clear away all the homeless people from the streets. There was something called the September Purge a couple of years ago when loads of people living rough got taken away to God knows where in an effort to 'keep the city clean'.

But so many now have nowhere to live that they've crept back again, especially since all the floods. The authorities seem to think that herding them into different areas is better than having no control at all.

Some of the tents here look quite decent. A woman with

long black hair and papery, crinkled skin is standing outside the nearest one, tending to a camping stove. A smell of curry wafts towards me, reminding me a little of Mum's Jamaican cooking. I stop for a second, smiling at the memory. Man, she packed so many Scotch bonnets into her food that grown men had been known to cry at the first mouthful.

The smile slips from my face. This is the first time I've thought about Mum in ages. And that doesn't seem right. It's like I'm forgetting her.

Sometimes it seems like there have been two Kylas, the one before Scotland and the one after. The woman glares at me and I decide to move on. Maybe she thinks I feel superior to her when, at this exact minute, she couldn't be more wrong. I'm picturing her pulling her kids, in their sleeping bags, in close each night for warmth, maybe whispering stories in their ears. I feel a weird tug of envy. They are together; connected. Part of a whole.

Me? No one cares if I live or die.

Wow, I'm in a weird place tonight.

I quicken my pace, heading towards Waterloo Bridge, dodging the war veterans you see busking everywhere now. There's a broken bit of railing about halfway along, and I make sure I give it a wide berth. You hear of people chucking themselves through that gap. It doesn't seem as though anyone is in a hurry to mend it, so maybe the authorities like keeping it that way. Fewer homeless people on the streets and all that.

There are blokes in wheelchairs juggling light balls, and a guy with a facial mask is singing some Scottish song in a high, wavering voice. There are more penny-whistle players than I can be bothered to count. Some of the ex-soldiers have no obvious injuries but there is a look I'm starting to recognise. It's partly the short haircut, but also the deadness in the eyes. I shudder and hurry on across the bridge, glancing over at the Gherkin, whose broken windows reflect the lights from police helicopters that swoop above the city. You get used to the sound after a while.

Same with the buzz drones that float and wind above the heads of people walking along, minding their own business. I still hate those things, with their fly-like eyes, which whirr and snap a zillion images a minute of the people below.

It's different here. Not like Sheffield. People were suspicious there, don't get me wrong. But you'd still get chatty folk in shops or on the bus. Yorkshire people like a natter, even when it can be a dangerous pastime.

In London, it's like danger is always just under the surface. You can almost taste fear in the air, along with the stink of cars and that toxic swamp that passes for a river. Maybe it's because London is the place that gets bombed the most.

I clamber up the steps, watching commuters in their miasma masks streaming the other way towards Waterloo Station. Heads down over phones, or just down. It sometimes feels like the whole city is staggering about under a massive weight of worry and sadness.

I walk down the steps at the far end, past the front of Embankment Station and head into Victoria Gardens. There's another Tent City here, this one a designated area for young professionals. It's for people in their late teens and early twenties who have jobs but nowhere to live. Music drifts from a couple of tents and I hear a burst of raucous laughter. There's a bit of a party atmosphere and the smell of weed starts to tickle my nose. I can feel a sneeze building up and I try to breathe it away but something has got through the mask and suddenly it feels like it's choking me . . .

I snatch the mask off my face, panicky for no reason I can put my finger on, breathing deeply. That's when I get a creeping sensation. It's one of the things I can do since being at CAT Camp; sense when someone is looking at me. And I don't just mean that hairs-up-on-the-back-of-the-neck thing that everyone has.

This is a certainty, deep in my bones, that someone is watching.

I haven't been wrong yet. I look around quickly but can't see anyone who looks suspicious. Just people going in and out of tents, clutching bottles.

I walk quickly away, not paying attention to where I'm going. I'm in too much of a hurry to put the mask back on at first. But as my throat starts to itch and tighten, I quickly pull it on, flipping my hood up and over my head. Traffic thunders by on Victoria Embankment as I walk quickly along the pavement. I don't want to look panicky by turning back the way I came, so am aiming for 'purposeful' instead. Not sure I'm succeeding, though. I reckon I'll make my way along to Blackfriars Bridge, cross the river and then head back to the flat.

Could be any number of reasons why someone was watching me, I tell myself. Maybe I imagined it? I've had a long day. I might be off my game. And I'm trying not to think about Adem. But I know I'm kidding myself. There's no mistaking the prickle and swoop in my guts that alerts me to danger. Maybe it was some sleazebag, liking what he saw? But I don't really think it was that either.

I'm hurrying along, trying to work it out, when I suddenly feel it again. I spin round, ready to take on whoever it is. But all I see is a smattering of homeless men, moving like satellites towards the odd miasma-masked commuter, asking for change and being ignored. No one seems to give me a second glance. I look across the road towards the river at people going the opposite way. Same. But wait . . .there's a tall bloke there, hooded and masked like me. He's walking this way and staring straight ahead but there's something . . .

I can't put my finger on what it is but I feel uneasy. I start walking sharply the other way and I see him stop and then try to dodge traffic to head in the same direction.

So you are following me, I think, a bit triumphant that I'm right, even though this isn't a good situation. He's having trouble getting across the road and I see his head turned towards me, definitely watching now. I cheekily give him the finger. He's having to wait for the lights to change so I've got plenty of time to get away now. I can walk away and never see him again; never find out who it was and what he wanted.

So of course I don't do that sensible thing. I'm curious about who he is and what he wants. When I see that his head is turned the other way, I turn sharply right into a road called Temple Place, that has some private, locked gardens. The gate into the gardens is set a little way back from the road so I press myself into it until I'm, hopefully, out of sight. Before too long I see him. He's about six feet tall, slim build. Maybe young. I can't tell. He glances up the road and I push myself back, heart pounding, and then he stops. A couple of people pass him but he stands dead still. I try not to breathe, even though the city noises are at their usual pitch; traffic and horns beeping, sirens from the boats on the Thames and the odd blast of music from one of the few cars that keeps its windows open. Not to mention the frequent, low-level hum of passing buzz drones. My heart feels as though it's going to burst out of my chest now but the figure moves off and I feel my knees go a little weak.

I know for a fact now that he was following me. But who was he and what did he want?

And then a thought creeps in before I can help it.

Cal?

Could it be him?

My legs go even wobblier. Do I even *want* it to be him?

I try to untangle the different thoughts that crowd my brain now.

OK, so he's probably dead. There was a, what, one in six chance he survived that bombing? But those aren't great odds. And if he did survive, wouldn't his parents being killed send him even further into the clutches of Torch? This makes me feel sick to my stomach.

No. It wasn't Cal. This was someone much older and taller. I'm letting my imagination get away with me. Much better that Cal is dead and innocent than alive and involved in terrorism.

When I get back to the flat I can't settle to anything. Phoenix has left and a girl called Maisie is there, along with Jake, a slightly older guy. We don't chat much. Everyone exchanges a handful of words then goes off and does their own thing. I take a mug of hot chocolate into the communications room to get the boring business of writing up my report over with.

There are several high-end computers in here that can be programmed into buzz-drone-like activity if you want to look at anything, along with others that are routed through hundreds of different servers to keep anonymity.

I'm about to open a document when I get an idea and head over to the CCTV terminals. I tap into the system. I only have very limited rights on it but this is one of the few things people at my level are allowed to do. Quickly locating the Embankment in *maps*, I tap in a rough time-window for when I was there.

I can't be bothered to watch the virtual 3D screen, so I just look at the terminal, watching people come and go. I speed it up because it's pretty boring, and then I see myself, coming out of Victoria Gardens. I slow it right down, watching myself being watched. It feels strange but I can't help being impressed at how casual I look. I felt jumpy but you wouldn't think I knew I was being followed, apart from the fact that I'm hurrying a little.

Then I see him, the tall figure, walking along on the other side of the road. He walks purposefully but could easily have caught up if he wanted to. Every now and then he glances my way, checking I'm still there. He seems to be working something out . . . maybe making a decision about whether to approach me. Then I have a chilling thought. What if it's the brother, son, nephew – whatever – of Stevie, the nursery worker who got carted away because of me? Or maybe it's someone from the job I just left?

Maybe Adem? But surely, even with the hood and mask, I would have recognised Adem straight away? Despite my doubts, though, I can't help feeling a little glow of hope inside at the thought that it might have been him. But, if it was him, how could he have found me? And if he's alive, he might want revenge . . .

'Operative name, please.'

The sudden voice in the room makes me yelp in shock. I

turn to the monitor next to me to see the face of my immediate boss, Ray. He was called a 'line manager' by someone, which was too ridiculous to be true. Sounds like he works in a bank. But anyway, Ray's job is to dole out the jobs. He seems to have no sense of humour at all and talks in a dull, monotone voice that must drive his wife nuts. Although he probably doesn't have a wife *to* drive nuts.

'It's Kyla, um, K66651,' I say, hurriedly remembering my operative number.

'Thank you,' says Ray, looking down and tapping something into another keyboard. He makes me wait for a few minutes, annoyingly, which I think is a bit of a power thing. Just showing me who's the boss and all that.

'Have you filed your report on job number CTR716 yet?' he says, without looking up.

'Just about to,' I say, trying not to sound irritated.

'Good,' he says, looking up and meeting my eye for the first time. 'Get it done quickly please because I have a new job for you.'

'Oh?' My insides seem to droop. I was hoping for a proper rest between jobs. To catch up on my sleep, go running. Eat . . .

'Are you listening?'

'Yes,' I say, stifling a sigh. 'Fire away.'

Then I think about what happened in the last job I did and I regret my choice of words.

CHAPTER 18

laura

My next job sounds easy enough.

Torch spend a lot of time hacking into government computers. Every now and then the massive 3D banners that roll across buildings showing the news will cut to messages designed to disrupt everything. They make up a load of lies and even show images that are obviously fake just to stir up unrest.

But to do this requires a huge amount of processing power, way beyond anything you can buy as a regular punter. So it's thought they have been building some kind of supercomputer system that uses the chips from old tablets, phones, computers, whatever. No one knows where it is but CAT are desperate to destroy it. By law everyone has to take their old phones and electronics to a government-approved site before they can buy anything new. If someone is found carrying old devices, they are immediately under suspicion.

My job is to follow a girl who has been seen with a bag containing what looks like several old tablets. It was called in by someone in the café where she works. There's a reward for this sort of information and some people make a living out of being snoops. Not that I judge them. I just get paid more for doing the same thing.

I'm told to watch her movements after she finishes her shift. Chat to her if I need to. There won't be a job there, so there's no point trying to get taken on as staff. Café and restaurant jobs are highly sought after these days. I decide to go into the café and order a coffee when I'm told she'll be working.

The café is on a road next to Hampstead Heath, which used to be a big park, I'm told. Now it's a smaller one, with half of it covered in warehouses. There are shops and cafés along the main road there. I'm looking for one called Antonio's.

I don't like taking the Tube, not since there was a plaster bomb at Oxford Circus, but it would take hours from here on the bus so I have no choice.

There are lots of power cuts on the Tube too so you'll be hurtling through a tunnel and then all the lights will go out. The emergency generators sometimes come on and that's almost as bad. All the faces take on a yellowish, sickly colour that's only a bit less spooky than the old holding-a-torch-under-the-chin trick Jax used to love doing.

Maybe I'll never be a true Londoner.

But it goes OK and the train only stops for about fifteen minutes (lights on, thank God) between Chalk Farm and Belsize Park.

The escalator at Hampstead Station is broken so I trudge up the metal steps and out into the muggy, damp air. The rain has stopped for a little while and the sun is nudging out from behind a cloud, throwing glints of gold onto roads slick with dirt and rain. I check my phone for directions and then make my way up a road in the direction of the café.

It doesn't take long. The café looks quite cosy, with a red and white striped awning that's only a bit grubby and tatty. There are a few plastic tables and chairs outside that are flecked with dirt and fat raindrops that look like bubble wrap.

Inside the café I immediately spot the girl, Laura Woods. She's standing at the counter, chatting to an older woman who expertly works an old-fashioned espresso machine that hisses and spits like a metal monster. I study a plastic menu, eyeing her at the same time. She's a little older than me, I think. Maybe seventeen. Her shiny blond hair is twisted into one of those sideways up-dos and she has a pencil neatly shoved through it. She wears glasses and has bright brown eyes and a big smile. She wears a little apron over a mini dress and boots. Pretty. And normal looking, I think. But that doesn't mean she isn't a filthy traitor.

She gets a text and turns away to read it. Her cheeks flush and she gives a little smile. It's a dead giveaway that someone special has sent it. She quickly tucks the phone into her pocket, pushes a strand of loose hair behind her ear and comes over to my table.

'Get you something?' she says. Although she is smiling, her mind is somewhere else, probably with whoever sent that text. She still doesn't look like someone who might be a terrorist but I'll keep an eye on her, anyway. After the last one, this is a nice easy job. I reckon I deserve it.

I order a hot chocolate and a muffin. I'm still tired from all those nights in Hoxton Mansions. I need a sugar boost.

Laura is coming to the end of her shift soon so I have just enough time to drink the hot chocolate and eat the muffin before I see her disappear out the back. I pay and leave, before finding a spot to watch the café. I pretend to window-shop at the bookshop across the road, where I can see the reflection of the café door opposite. After a few minutes she comes out, wearing a leather jacket over the dress. She's fluffed out her hair a bit and put on some lipstick.

She looks along the street in both directions before moving away. Unless she's waiting for someone, it seems a bit strange. Maybe she does have something to hide, after all. She doesn't put on a miasma mask but it's not too bad today, after the rain.

Laura walks away in the direction of the park, up a road lined with grand houses that have tropical plants in bright jewel colours spilling over balconies.

She looks around now and then, but I'm sure she hasn't spotted me. I keep a careful distance.

After a few minutes Laura turns into the entrance to the park. The sky darkens and seems to clear its throat as thunder rumbles above. A few drops of rain splash onto the path around my feet. She's obviously meeting someone. And that's when she does a sort of patting thing to her handbag, like she's double checking she has it. Interesting. Maybe she has something to hide in there. Like an old phone or two?

As Laura heads up the hill inside the Heath I snap open an umbrella and reach for my phone. Pretending to chat to someone (I even let out the odd giggle for authenticity), I never take my eyes off her. A few dog-walkers and cyclists pass and I avoid eye contact.

Just as she reaches the top of the hill, Laura does a three-sixty look around. I turn the other way and talk into my phone in an animated way. Her eyes brush over me and then move on. I follow, slowly now.

There's someone sitting on a bench at the very top of the hill. A young bloke, with a rain jacket on. The hood is up. They hug and he pulls away first. She sits down very close to him on the bench but he doesn't put his arm around her or anything. Maybe this date isn't going to go the way she's hoping.

I stand under the umbrella at a distance, wondering how I might get a better look without being seen. I could walk by. Maybe I'll ask directions back to the station, although they'll wonder why I don't just use my phone.

They're having quite an animated conversation now. The girl raises her voice and although I can't catch what she's saying, the mood has changed, I can tell. I want to get closer so, lowering my gaze, I start yabbering a load of rubbish into the phone, like, 'Shut up! You are such a liar! Come on, tell me what really happened,' and 'I don't *believe* you sometimes!' The kind of stuff I imagine normal girls my age might say to each other. Like I'd know.

Laura is on her feet now.

'I don't think I want to help any more,' she says in a tight voice. 'I've had enough.'

I aim for a casual walk past the bench. She glances at me and I keep my eyes down, laughing like I've just heard a great joke, only letting my eyes graze the scene when I'm directly level with them.

And then the boy is on his feet, crying something out.

And I realise what I've heard is my own name.

And then I think, *How can he know my name?*

And then I understand who I'm looking at.

Cal.

Alive.

CHAPTER 19

terrorist

I stare and stare, my brain refusing to believe what I'm seeing.

I let the wind snatch the umbrella from my hand. Images come crashing into my head: bombs going off. People getting hurt. Torch. Torch are to blame. Is Cal with Torch? Is he a terrorist? Is this why he's meeting up with a suspect?

I can't speak. We stare at each other. His lips are parted; his eyes full of confusion and something else. Happiness? As if it's that simple . . .

'Oh, I get it,' says Laura.

Is she still here?

'I'm such an idiot,' she continues. 'Why didn't you just say there was someone else instead of stringing me along?'

Cal ignores her. So do I. But as shakes begin to travel up

from my feet and into my limbs, I feel a sense of dread and terror that makes me want to be sick. It's all wrong.

My face throbs. I'm hot inside, like I'm going to explode.

I don't know what to do. What to think.

So I turn and run.

I see my umbrella blowing and bouncing down the hill, turning and twisting like a prehistoric black bird.

I can't breathe. I can't think straight. All I want to do is run and not stop. The whole universe has cracked right open and doesn't make sense any more.

Footsteps pound behind me. He's shouting my name.

'Kyla! Kyla, stop!'

I'm a fast runner but he's faster than me. The footsteps get closer and closer until I feel a cold, strong hand grabbing my wrist.

And I turn and hit him, hard, in the face. I don't know why I do it. It's pure instinct at being grabbed. But maybe it's the fact that the word 'terrorist', 'terrorist' is screaming in my mind, over and over.

He gasps and touches his lip where I've thumped him. It's puffy. He looks down at the blood on his fingers.

'Kyla?' he says and there's a cracking in his voice, like he wants to cry or something. 'Why did you hit me?'

This question takes me by surprise for some reason. But the one I was expecting comes next.

'Why did you run away?'

Confusion swamps me with the strength of a tsunami.

I gulp, trying to hold it back. All the fight in me melts away like it was never there. I start to cry and a painful kind of hope starts to spread through my belly and up into my chest. I bow my head and he steps forward, tentatively. His arms snake around me then, strong and warm. I smell the rain and chill in his jacket and bury my face into it. My head only comes up to his chest now. Last time he held me, I reached his shoulder. He's broader too. Not the boy he was but a young man. And I know. It was him I saw, watching me before.

I can feel the shakes in his body as he holds me. He's whispering, 'Kyla, Kyla,' so softly it's more like I sense it than hear it.

I keep my eyes closed, wishing I could stay where I am and not have to think about the next second, minute, hour, lifetime.

'Cal?'

Laura is standing next to us and Cal quickly pulls away. He blushes and looks flustered at the sight of this rain-drenched girl.

'Oh,' he says, hoarsely. He clears his throat. 'I'm sorry. This isn't why, though. I wasn't lying before.'

Laura snorts loudly. 'Yeah, RIGHT,' she says. Then she moves in closer. Her eyes are wild. 'I'm done here. If you think I'll help any more after this, and put myself in danger for your stupid cause then you can *piss right off*.' She gulps a sob as Cal tries to speak.

'Laura, I'm sorry, I never —'

She swears at him in a hiss and then stalks away, pulling her leather jacket closer and hunching in on herself.

Cal turns back to me. We stare at each other for I don't know how long. Everything feels hazy and unreal, despite the rain thundering down around us and dripping off our faces and chins. And all we can do is look.

After a moment he says, 'I can't believe it's really you.' He reaches out a hand as though to touch me and then lets it drop.

I'm getting colder and colder by the second. I start to shake, gently at first and then my body is almost convulsing. I have a headache that clutches my scalp like fingers that are at once ice cold then seem to burn through to my skull.

'Kyla?' Cal comes closer. His face seems too big, distorted, like it has been reflected by some weird mirror. 'Are you OK? You look a bit . . . sick.'

'I'm all right,' I say through gritted teeth as goose pimples prickle up my arms and my vision does a complete three-sixty spin. I clench my fists together and press them to my sides. I don't know what I might do with them because even though I want to grab Cal and kiss the lovely face off him – clinging on and never letting him out of my sight again – it's like someone is whispering in my ear. Three words, over and over again.

Terrorist.

and

KILL HIM . . .

The world spins and I stagger sideways. Cal grabs my arm in a strong grip and puts his arm around me, stopping me from falling.

'Come on, let's get out of the rain so we can talk,' he says quietly. I'm feeling too pathetic to argue.

I lean into him, still violently shaking, as we head towards the gate.

I don't pay much attention to where we go. I know I should but I tell myself that if I don't know where he lives, then I'm under no obligation to tell anyone. But I *should* tell someone, shouldn't I? I'm so confused.

We end up getting two Tube trains. On the second one, the train slows ominously and then stops in a tunnel. We're plunged into darkness and the anxiety filling the air spreads like a bad smell.

I feel so weird. My mouth is dry and my hands keep sweating. I seem to be able to sense every inch of Cal next to me. His leg is right by mine. I can feel the heat of him rising from his damp jeans and seeping into my skin. I look down at his hand, resting on his knee, and see that the skin is all puckered and white. Burned.

I look away.

We haven't spoken since we got onto the train.

I can't seem to find any words to say. Maybe it's the same for him. I've never felt such a weird mix of emotions. There's a sense of something terrible coming, and then short bursts of total, happy, fling-your-arms-up-and-cheer joy. I'm all mixed up, churning, inside. My head's not straight.

And we've been sitting here too long. Has something . . . Oh God, has something happened? Maybe there has been a bomb somewhere on the line?

The emergency lights snap on and the sickly glow renders everyone with the same hollow-eyed, nervous expression. Smells of wet wool, stale breath and sweat creep further up my nose. It's too hot. Sweat prickles my neck and palms. There isn't enough air . . .

To distract myself from the panic rising inside I stare at our reflections in the window opposite. It's the first time I've been able to get a proper look at him.

His blond hair is shorter and darker than I remember from before, maybe dyed now? His face is more angular, older, and his eyes look like they have seen too much. Like mine, I guess. When I knew him before, he had a sort of innocence about him, plus a big laugh and a smile that lit up his eyes, despite all the shit he'd been through. Like none of it had spoiled the goodness inside. But what about now? What kind of things might he have taken part in if he's still with Torch?

Torch . . .

My body gives an involuntary shudder and Cal sits up quickly, concerned.

'Are you all right?' he says. I nod sharply and stare down at my soaked trainers, willing myself to keep it together. Maybe I should get off at the next stop and just run away, pretend I never saw him. But even thinking that gives me a sharp pain in my ribs like someone has stabbed me in the heart. I want to, I want . . .

Kill him . . .

I yelp at the thought, which came complete in my ear as though someone hissed the words. Cal just reaches for my hand and squeezes. I look down at his long, pale fingers around my smaller brown one. I close my eyes and try to breathe slowly.

After a few more stops we get out somewhere I don't recognise. I force myself not to notice the name of the stop although I can't help seeing it's *Something* Grove.

There is a long walk up a path enclosed by fences from the station. People walk with heads down against the rain. We don't speak as we walk past a row of boarded-up shops. A launderette. A newsagent's. An Indian restaurant with broken windows. I find myself trying to memorise the names and then I force myself to stop. It's automatic now. I can't seem to help it.

After some time we turn left into a street lined with trees. The houses are all the same: red brick with bay windows and layers of slates on the front that are generally cracked or missing in places. They remind me of broken teeth. I feel Cal become more alert, like his muscles are coiled and ready for attack. But soon we stop outside a house with completely dark windows. Cal puts a key in the lock and turns it and gives me a reassuring smile as we step into a bright hallway.

I quickly see that the front door is covered in thick, light-absorbing material.

We turn into a living room with a big bay window covered in the same material.

A fitness video game is playing, too loud, and the bouncy American woman in 3D screeches about crunches and thrusts to an otherwise empty room. Cal goes over to turn it off and then goes back into the hall, opening a door and then returning with two thin, threadbare towels, their colour long since faded into grey nothing.

We stare at each other again for a minute. I'm so cold now from being wet through my teeth chatter. I dab at my face with the towel. He looks freezing too. The tip of his nose and his cheeks are a bit red and for a second it seems like the sweetest thing I've ever seen. I start to gently dry my face, wishing I was touching his instead.

He does the same and our eyes lock together. I'm tingling all over. The dizziness and the evil voice in my ear have gone away now. Everything has shrunk down to this room; us standing here, so close. Cold and hot all at once.

Then he breaks out into a huge grin and pulls me towards him. And we're kissing and laughing all at once and I feel like a bottle of Coke that has been shaken up and is about to explode inside me.

It's all going to be OK now. This is *Cal*. How could I even think about hurting him?

We sit down on a sofa that has tiny scratches all over it, like a cat has been using it as a claw-sharpening post. It's lumpy and uncomfortable and springs dig into my legs and back.

There's so much to say, I don't know where to start and, I think, neither does he. But I speak first.

'How did you survive the bomb and . . . ?' I whisper.

I don't finish the sentence. He grimaces and looks down, clenching his hand into a fist. His voice is low and trembles with emotion when he finally speaks.

'Sam wanted to get some champagne to celebrate me meeting . . .' He pauses and I see his Adam's apple bob as he swallows deeply before continuing, '. . . my parents.' Another pause. 'Said there was an old bottle in that little cupboard in the kitchen. He wanted to go but I said I'd get it. I was feeling a bit overwhelmed and needed a few minutes.' He delivers the words as though they're hurting his mouth. 'I could hear Julia talking to them. Everyone was laughing. Sort of nervous laughter, but happy. And . . .' he sucks in a great draught of shuddery air, 'the next thing I knew, I was deaf. Everything was dark. I hurt everywhere. And something was on top of me.'

He pauses, staring down at the ground. I feel like I should comfort him but I don't know how.

Cal clears his throat and gives a shaky sigh. 'Remember that massive old table in the kitchen?'

I nod. It was big enough to seat about twenty people, carved from heavy, dark wood.

'Well, it saved my life. I was wedged underneath. Two of

the legs had come off but it was covering me so I only got a bit injured. I was lucky . . .'

My eyes creep to his scarred hand and he must sense it because he shifts and pulls the sleeve down a bit further.

We sit in silence. Then an image flashes into my mind. It's the farmhouse seen in 3D projection during the HT lesson at camp. A sharp pain prods between my eyeballs, like someone is pinching me there, squeezing.

'Kyla?'

I jolt, realising Cal is frowning at me.

'Yeah, yeah,' I say quickly. 'What did you do then? After?'

Cal looks off into the distance, biting his lip. His brown eyes glistening a little. 'Nathan had been away that day, do you remember?'

I nod, even though I don't really. And the name 'Nathan' causes a spasm of bright light to bloom inside my mind. Explosions . . . people being hurt.

Who's to blame, Kyla?

Voices in my head. But Cal doesn't notice. Just carries on talking.

'Anyway, he came back that night. Got me out and helped me get patched up.'

He lifts his sleeve then. His whole right arm is puckered and scarred. I wince. I'm trying to concentrate but the strange buzzing in my ears is distracting me. I shake my head, trying to clear it.

It takes me a second to realise Cal is speaking again.

'. . . and then I ended up down here.' He laughs suddenly. 'I still can't believe it's really you! I wondered. I even thought I'd seen you the other day.'

I don't respond. Maybe it was him. I don't want to tell him; I don't know why.

There's a rapid-fire sound of footsteps down stairs then. A lanky bloke in his twenties with stringy blond hair comes into the room at top speed and then brakes suddenly, his eyes on me.

'Who's this?' he says to Cal. His voice is high and tight; suspicious.

'It's OK,' Cal says, jumping to his feet with his hand raised. 'It's the girl I told you about, Kyla. She's alive!'

The other bloke moves closer. His eyes are narrowed into slits and his body seems coiled. I feel as though he's smelling my intentions, like a dog. My hands start to shake uncontrollably and the buzzing ups in volume. I can't look at the bloke or Cal. I feel like something really bad will happen if I do.

I stare instead at the low table in front of me that's made from bricks and a slab of wood. There are plates smeared with colours that make me think of blood. A single sock. Someone's game controller. My feet are planted side by side in front of me on the scruffy carpet and I try to concentrate on them.

'What's wrong with her? Why is she rocking like that?'

I'm *rocking*?

But I'm in the dark place now. I hurt. There's too much pain and noise.

Another harsh voice comes from the end of a long, long tunnel.

Enemy ... Kill the enemy ... Wipe out Torch ...

I flap my hands at my ears to make the words go away. Then my hand seems to creep towards my right trainer, like it has a life of its own.

'Kyla?' Cal's voice is distant, like something half-remembered.

It has to stop ... Stop the pain ...

The other bloke is talking, louder. The words are almost distorted.

'Look, mate, I'm happy you've found your old girlfriend but she's a liability, she can't stay h—'

He doesn't finish the sentence, though.

Because I've pulled the blade from the sole of my trainer and I'm lunging at his throat.

CHAPTER 20

we don't do things that way

Shouting. Movement. Pain.

I'm tossed face-down onto the smelly sofa, arms wrenched behind my back. I can't breathe. Lots of people seem to be yelling at the same time so none of it makes sense. Something is grinding into the base of my spine as my hands get tied. A knee. But I feel weirdly distant from what's happening to me. I think I just tried to stab that man. Did that really happen?

The buzzing in my ears comes back. I think I might be sick, face down here. I'll choke. Pure terror blasts through the numb feeling and I shake uncontrollably. If I could crawl out of my own skin right now, I would. If I could choose to die, I would.

I don't even recognise myself in this girl who just tried to stab someone.

I'm flipped back round the other way like a rag doll. The back of my head thumps against the hard wall above the sofa. I'm looking up at the bloke I attacked. He straddles me, his weight pushing down on my bound arms behind my back. It *hurts*. His eyes are beaming hate, but fear too. I recognise it now, when anger is a thin layer over what's really there.

'Who the hell *are* you?' he snarls. There's spit at the corners of his lips. A livid purple spot seems to shine from his forehead. All the details of his face are too brightly lit.

Cal, just behind him, stares down at me with an expression that makes my guts curl into a tight knot.

I almost *murdered* someone. But it was like I had no choice. I *had* to do it. Like it was the thing I'd been born to do.

But already that powerful feeling is hard to grasp, like a dream that slips away when you wake up. I squeeze my eyes closed, confusion and shock pumping through me.

'Who sent you? Are you a CATS' Eye?'

There's no point in lying any more.

I nod slowly.

Cal makes a sound; it's part groan, part gasp. Then he stumbles backwards, his eyes wide and round.

I hear the crash of the front door shortly afterwards.

The other man roughly cuts off my tracker watch and takes it away.

Shortly after, the door opens and closes. More voices fill the hallway.

I keep re-living how it felt with the blade in my hand. I was seconds away from being a killer. Seconds. Tears rise up inside then and I hide my face in my knees. I'm not looking for sympathy. Probably wouldn't get it now anyway, even from Cal. He had everything taken away from him by the people I work for.

Worked for? I don't know what tense to use. I don't know where I belong. I wish I could crawl away and hide under a stone. It feels like what I deserve. Stuff that seemed so clear cut this morning is cloudy and blurred now. I was so *sure*. How can I have been so sure I was right?

'Here, drink this,' says a rough voice. I look up through bleary, sore eyes into a bearded face I recognise. It's Nathan. I flinch. He always did look permanently angry and now is no exception. He should have little devil horns and red eyes, considering how I'd been seeing him and his kind for the last six months. But all I see is a tall, skinny bloke with a beard and a T-shirt with a rip in the sleeve. Not a devil. Just an exhausted-looking man.

He's holding a cup of water. I eye it with suspicion.

He tuts, loudly. 'It's only water. We don't do things the way your friends do.'

I lean in and take a sip, avoiding his dark, angry eyes, which seem to jab holes in my skin.

He stands up again and I glance around the room. The guy I tried to stab is sitting on the opposite sofa. Nathan stands back, regarding me. A pretty woman with blond hair swept into a curly ponytail comes into the room. She does the eye skewer thing too.

'Where's Cal?' she says.

'Gone for a walk,' says the man whose name I still don't know, despite the intimacy of having almost taken his life. 'Needed to clear his head, as you can imagine.'

'I can't believe he brought someone back here!' says the woman, her voice rising in fury.

'He knows her,' says Nathan quietly. 'She's special to him.' He pauses. 'Or was.'

The words do exactly what they were intended to do. I close my eyes, wincing, and lower my head again.

'Are you sure you're all right, Dan?' says the woman.

'Yeah. I could tell something was weird about her,' says the bloke I tried to hurt. 'Still took me by surprise, though.'

'When I think what could have . . .' The woman bites off the end of her sentence. I don't know if Dan is her boyfriend but I don't blame her for hating me. I can almost feel her self-control in not going for me. I almost wish she would.

'The question is, what are we going to do with her now?' says the man called Dan. 'She knows this address. She's a liability. Best thing would be to chuck her in the Thames.'

'Stop it,' says Nathan sharply. 'We're better than that, remember?'

The tiny sliver of kindness in his voice reaches inside me.

Nathan walks over and squats down in front of me, looking right into my eyes.

'Kyla, I remember you. And I'm very surprised at what you have become. I need to ask you something very important, OK?'

I nod, a bit bewildered by where this is going.

'Where did they train you?'

I'm so confused by the question I don't answer. He continues. 'Was it Birmingham? Or Cardiff?'

My lips move but no sound comes out. It feels wrong to tell them, despite everything. Like something bad will happen if I let the word out.

'What?' he says gently. 'What did you say?'

'*Scotland.*' The word rides on my breath like a sigh.

There's a pause.

'Was it a place called . . . Area Six?'

I hang my head and then nod once. I don't want to talk about any of that.

'Oh, dear God,' says Nathan heavily and swipes his face with a meaty hand. He rocks back on his heels and then gets to his feet, huffing a little. 'You poor kid.'

'What is it?' The blond woman asks sharply.

'I've heard what they do there,' says Nathan. 'They call it *Commitment Training.*' He pauses. 'We would call it brainwashing.'

The word makes me flinch.

'*Brainwashing?*' says Dan.

Nathan heaves a heavy sigh and gets up, before sitting down on the opposite chair. He leans forwards and clasps his hands between his knees. He studies me so intently, I feel like an exhibit in a glass case.

'What do you remember about it?' he says, ignoring Dan.

I try to find the words for something that's buried so deep, you'd need a surgeon's knife to get to it.

'I know they did something,' I say shakily. 'In fact, they did it twice. I don't really remember too much. The rest of the time we were just taught to do useful stuff.'

He nods. 'And after this . . . *something*,' he says, 'what did you feel about us? About Torch?'

My sight blurs as tears crowd and drip down my hot cheeks. 'I hated you,' I whisper. 'I hated you and I was trained to kill you.'

'And now, Kyla?' says Nathan. 'Do you still want to kill us?'

I look up and meet his eyes then shake my head emphatically, side to side. It's the truth. I don't. It's crazy, but I don't. How can things have changed so suddenly?

'Come on,' says Dan to Nathan, scornfully. 'You're not serious about this?'

Nathan looks at him. 'I'm deadly serious. It might surprise you to know that in the last five years they've been reprising and improving some of the basic techniques that have been around since the 1950s.'

'What sort of *techniques*?' says the woman. She sounds scornful and I see her exchange a loaded look with Dan.

Nathan grimaces. 'Sensory deprivation, disorientation. Drugs. Repeated negative imagery. Lack of sleep. The CIA had a major programme called MK-ULTRA for about thirty years. They explored just about every aspect of brainwashing. Even back in the 2010s they were using the drug Sodium Pentothal on Al Qaeda suspects.'

'Why?' says Dan sharply. 'What does that do?'

'They tried it as a truth drug,' he says. 'But it didn't work that well. The idea was that you got the subject into a raw state with all the other techniques and then opened up their minds with the drug. I've heard they've developed things a little since then.'

He looks at Dan. 'There's a thing called the Box. They keep them in absolute darkness so they are disorientated. Drug them up. Then they bombard them with imagery and give them shocks. It's nasty stuff, from what I've heard.'

Everyone stares at me. Silence cloaks the room.

Those bastards *brainwashed* me?

No wonder I felt so strange for so long . . . like I'd lost a piece of myself and couldn't get it back. And now? I don't even know what to feel now, except that I can't stand all their eyes on me. I'm not on any 'side' now, am I? I don't even know who the good guys really are any more. I stare miserably down at the purple carpet, which is pocked with crusty fag burns and crumbs.

'So what the hell do we do with her now?' says Dan after a few minutes. 'Is she still dangerous?'

I look up and meet Nathan's eyes.

'No,' he says quietly. 'I don't believe so. I've heard that the effects of the brainwashing are only temporary. That's why so many CATS' Eyes get eliminated after they stop being useful.'

Eliminated?

I suck in my breath. Nathan sighs.

'I don't suppose they made that clear in your,' he makes air quotes with his fingers, '*training*, did they?' He runs his hand over his beard and blows out air again. 'The brainwashing is intense and effective ... temporarily. It can be undone by a bout of sickness, certain medicines ... possibly even by emotional stress or shocks. CATS' Eyes are what's known as "expendable". I've never heard of a one who has worked for longer than a year at most.'

'What happens after that?' My lips feel stiff and strange. But I have to know.

Nathan shrugs. Then speaks again. 'I feel very sorry for you, Kyla, for what it's worth.'

A flicker of hope flares inside.

'But I'm afraid it is a risk we can't take,' says Nathan. The hope is replaced by a stab of cold fear. 'We'll have to move on. Dismantle everything here and find somewhere else. And you,' he says, looking down at me, 'can't stay.'

'I won't say anything.' I sound young and pathetic, like I'm promising not to tell on the person who stole the last biscuit.

'We're not taking that chance!' snaps the woman. 'I'll have to take you away to make sure you're gone.'

I cringe into myself. My tough shell seems to have cracked. I want to see Cal. I also don't want to see him. I keep remembering his face when he left. Like I disgusted him.

I don't want to go anywhere with her, anyway. Thankfully Nathan comes to my rescue.

'She's as much a victim as Dan nearly was, so I'll thank you to calm down a bit. Isn't this what we are for? To try to fight back against a regime that treats people like lab rats?' He runs his hand over his beard again. It's like a nervous tic. I remember he used to do this, but not as much. So many damaged people . . .

'Kyla, will you be expected to check in tonight?' He's all brisk efficiency now.

'No,' I say quietly. 'I'll have twenty-four hours' grace, because I'm meant to be on a . . . um, job.'

Dan makes a disgusted sound and the woman's face tightens even further. But it's clear Nathan is in charge.

I keep thinking about what we learned in History of Terrorism. Can it all have been lies? The words come bursting out of me, unexpectedly.

'They told me *you* are behind all those attacks. Torch.'

Nathan regards me and sighs heavily. 'Of course they did.'

We all turn at the sound of the front door opening and closing. Cal comes into the room. The rain must have stopped. Although his hair is still stuck to his face a little and his trainers are darkened around the toes, he isn't noticeably wetter than he was when he got back here. For a second I have a fierce, powerful wish that I hadn't come here. Hadn't found out about any of this. It was better, thinking he was dead. Simpler.

He can't even look at me now.

'You OK?' says Nathan brusquely. Cal looks dazed as he nods. 'Come on,' says Nathan, gesturing to Dan and the woman. 'Let's give them a minute to talk?'

Cal turns to him. 'It's OK,' he says coldly. 'I don't need to talk.'

I catch the eye of the blond woman and wish I hadn't. Her face is bright with malice. Cal's words hurt. He walks out of the room and Nathan looks at me and then shrugs.

'OK, well, I'm sure you'll understand, Kyla, that we have to take certain precautions. We don't want you wandering off before we're ready to let you go.'

He looks at the woman.

'Tilly,' he says, 'put her in that small bedroom at the back. And lock the door please.'

She almost clicks her fingers at me and I stiffen. I'm somehow coming back into myself. She'd better not touch me. I glare back at her, contemplating whether I should just run for the front door but I don't really have the strength for it. My limbs feel weak and wobbly. The shock of finding out that Cal is alive and then all those feelings being stirred up by him again, attacking Dan and then finding out what really happened to me in Scotland. Losing Cal again. Because I have. I know I have. It's all too much to take.

I muster as much dignity as I can and follow the woman called Tilly out of the room. I can just see a small kitchen at the end of the corridor where Cal is standing, his hands down on the counter and his head bent. He looks so sad, as though an unbearable weight is pressing on him. I want more than anything to be allowed to touch him but I know I never can again.

My eyes blur with hot tears.

I'm so sorry, I say, but only inside my head. No one wants to hear it. Being told about the brainwashing hasn't stopped the feeling of shame that I almost killed a man. Would I have tried to kill Cal too?

I follow Tilly miserably up the bare wooden stairs. The banister is splintery and rough under my fingers. We walk down a short landing past a few rooms and stop outside a bathroom. The door is open and I can see a bath that looks like some horrible green plastic. Better than the bathroom at the squat, but a far cry from the luxury at the flat. Expendable? Is that what I am?

'Do you need to go?' she says coldly. I nod, feeling stupidly ashamed again. She even comes in with me and I have to clench my fists not to lose my temper about the way she's enjoying me being a prisoner.

After, she slightly pushes my shoulder towards a room at the end of the corridor and I whirl round.

'I'm doing what you want,' I say in an icy voice. 'So keep your hands off me.'

We meet eyes. Hers are so cold and hard, I feel loneliness like a hollow ache in my stomach. I can tell she's dying to say something and then it bursts out of her.

'Why didn't you resist them?' she hisses. 'I wouldn't let them do that to me.'

I drop my eyes and ignore her. Maybe she's right. Maybe I was weak and pathetic and that's how they managed to turn me into a CATS' Eye. If Tilly had been in the situation I was in and had to make that choice, she would have taken prison. Well, bully for her.

'You wouldn't understand,' I mumble and she snorts.

'Clearly not,' she says and then unlocks the door in front of us.

I follow her in. It was obviously a kid's bedroom at one point because there's a line of painted animals around the middle of the wall and some tatty remnants of what looks like football stickers around the doorframe. The room is bare apart from a mattress on the floor, covered in a couple of blankets. Lace curtains the colour of old nicotine hang limply from the windows and the room smells musty and damp.

'Don't even think about going anywhere,' says Tilly. 'The windows are barred. Make no mistake, we don't want you here – but *we* will choose when you leave.' She stands a little straighter and her gaze scours me. She tuts. 'The truth is, you disgust me.'

She walks quickly out of the room and I hear the key clunk in the lock.

Join the queue, I think.

I sit down on the lumpy mattress, which is old but clean. I hold my hands, which are untied now, in front of my face and stare at them. My nails are clean and tipped white after having spent a night in the riverside flat. But they came close to being covered in that man's blood. I clench them into fists and press them into my eye sockets until crazy psychedelic colours swirl before me.

CHAPTER 21

their people

I 'm lying on the mattress with a rough blanket pulled over me. Grey daylight seeping through the curtains gradually begins to fade. The rain patters against the windows. There are other noises inside the house too. Quick footsteps and the sound of the front door opening and closing. I think they are moving out of this place. I wonder if they will leave me in here. It's hard to care all that much.

Curled in a ball, I try to ignore the smell from the blanket and after a while I start to shiver. I keep picturing how it felt when I lunged at Dan with the knife.

I wish I could make them understand that it wasn't my fault. If the farmhouse hadn't been bombed, I would have stayed and fought with Torch.

Should I have resisted what they did in Scotland? I'm

sure I couldn't have. But maybe I was just too tired to fight. All this goes round and round in my head and I start to feel angry again rather than afraid. Angry that Mum died. Angry that Zander turned me into a thief. Angry that Jax was taken from me. And angry that Cal has been taken from me again. Maybe some of my spark is still there inside. A weak spark, but there all the same.

After a while a woman I haven't seen before unlocks the door and gives me a tray with a plate of beans on toast and a mug of stewed orange tea. She stares at me as though I'm something in a zoo before carefully placing the tray on the floor and then scurrying away again.

I'm hungry, despite everything. I eat every last scrap, gulping down the metallic-tasting tea to the very bottom of the cup and holding it upside down to catch the dregs. Feeling sleepy then, I pull the smelly blanket around me again and close my eyes.

When I was little and something had scared me, my mum would say, 'Think of something happy, baby.' I'd scrunch my eyes tightly closed and remember ice lollies in the park, or the time we went to the Notting Hill Carnival and I sat on her shoulders, feeling like I was queen of all I could see, as noise and smells and colours whirled around me.

But too much has happened since then. I can't think of anything any more that would take me away from this. Maybe I stopped being capable of happiness a long time ago. Maybe I just don't deserve any. Still, as I drift off to sleep, the scene that plays through my mind is when Cal held me. A few hours ago. A lifetime ago.

I wake up with a jolt. My heart thrums against my ribs as my eyes adjust to the dark room. The pale glow of a streetlight seeps through the badly fitting curtains, which splash stripes of shadow on the wall opposite. A car alarm is wah-wahing somewhere in the street. Maybe that's what woke me.

My arms ache from where Dan pulled them behind me and I wince as I wriggle them in slow circles. A gentle knock at the door makes me stop, mid-movement.

I don't answer but watch as the door opens, feeling a weird sense of dread. For just a second, I'm convinced someone has come in here to kill me. I pull my knees up to my chest in a defensive ball but I haven't the stomach to fight any more.

'Kyla, are you awake?' says Cal quietly. I mumble an answer.

He sits down against the opposite wall, stretching his long legs out in front of him. The broken patch of light on the wall bathes half his face in shadow.

'You all right?'

I don't answer him. I literally have no idea how to talk to him after all that has happened.

He brings one knee up and rests his elbow on it, threading his fingers across his forehead. He's watching me. I'm self-conscious: unsure what to do with my limbs and hands. I clear my throat and pull my knees in closer to my chest, protecting myself, although from what, I'm not sure. I look at a patch of wall just past his face. It's easier than meeting the full beam of his gaze, dark though it is. It's like he's trying to work out who I am. I don't like how this feels.

'I understand about *hate*,' he says after a few moments of thick silence. I glance at him, confused and surprised by his words. 'It's what keeps me going sometimes,' he continues, 'the idea that we might beat these people someday. After what they did to me . . .' He pauses and I see him swallow. 'You see, I was lost for a while. I was completely alone in the world. Then I met you and Jax and I felt like I belonged somewhere, even if it was temporary.' He pauses. 'And even if it meant working for that creep Zander.'

I don't know what he wants me to say so I say nothing at all.

'And then they killed Jax . . .' He hesitates again. 'See, that's what I don't understand,' he says, his voice rising in volume. 'How you could join them after that? Can you help me *understand*?'

My eyes brim over and a hot tear skates down my cheek.

'So you don't get it either,' I say, and my voice is thick now. 'You think I chose for any of it to happen? I didn't choose to get brainwashed. Didn't Nathan explain about the brainwashing? That I'm a victim in all this too?'

He makes a dismissive noise. Angry heat creeps up my neck and cheeks. 'I can't make you believe me, Cal. Although I could tell you that I ended up in that place because I'd been arrested for attacking a man who wanted to rape me.' I hear him gasp at this and know I've hit home.

'What happened?' he says and I shake my head.

'It doesn't matter now. OK, I chose to go become a CATS' Eye rather than go to prison. But when I was there, I was brainwashed. And *you*, Cal Conway,' I jab a shaking finger in his direction, 'are the one person in the bloody world who *should* understand!'

'Why?' he says.

Fury surges up at how stubborn and thick he's being. I'm sick of feeling guilty. I couldn't help what they did to me. They were too powerful. I couldn't fight back.

'Because it was like what happened to *you*, you moron!' I yell. 'You of all people should understand that you can't fight back!' A new batch of tears threatens and I swallow them back angrily. 'And anyway,' I say fiercely, 'I'm sorry what happened to your parents but don't try to pretend that Torch are innocent too!'

'What do you mean?' he says and has the nerve to look bewildered.

'I *mean*,' I say in a hiss, 'that whatever Nathan says, I know plaster bombs were being stored in that house!'

For a moment he stares at me and then, when he speaks, his voice is as loud as mine has become. 'Yes and that's because a batch of government-approved devices had been stolen and kept there! Didn't you listen to anything? About how Tom and Julia had intercepted a shipment of bombs?

And how they were being kept until it could be decided what to do with them?'

A sudden sharp memory flashes into my mind. Me, staring into the fireplace, numb with grief as I thought about Jax. There were conversations going on around me. Something about bombs and a sense of celebration.

I drop my head into my hands and squeeze my eyes shut. I was so out of it after Jax died, I didn't really take in what was happening that much. But I know he is right. Cal isn't a liar. What you see is what you get with him. Unlike me.

'The government are the ones behind all the bombings of these past few years,' he says. 'They have all those old terrorist groups in their pockets now. Spreading panic and fear is big business. Think about how much money has been spent on personal security and private streets.' I can sense that these are Nathan's words he is speaking now, like he's reading a script. I think about Adem and Stevie from the nursery. How I helped them be caught. I squeeze my eyes shut. I'd like to scrub my skin with a wire brush until I bleed. And it still wouldn't be enough . . .

'So,' I say pathetically, 'why did they teach us how to disable them then?'

Cal rolls his eyes as though I've said something unbelievably dim. 'You have to understand what you're working with, don't you? Plaster bombs can go wrong or go off when they shouldn't. I expect they want their people to know how to handle them.'

Their people . . .

We sit in silence for several more minutes. I've never been so tired in my life. I wish I could close my eyes and make it all go away.

'So what's going to happen now?' I say eventually. I keep my eyes on my hands, which twist in my lap.

'This clearly isn't a safe house any more,' says Cal in an exhausted voice. 'So everyone has cleared out. I'm to wait here with you till morning so everyone has got time to get away properly. Nathan says it's lucky this happened now. It's so-called Freedom Day the day after tomorrow. All security attention will be on that.'

I'd forgotten what time of year it was.

Although any group of people larger than ten has been banned from meeting in public places since 2018 or something, once a year there is a so-called Celebration of Freedom. It's a total joke. There is usually some sort of demonstration that ends in violence and I can't imagine why anyone would bother going. But people like a party, even in 2024. And this is what passes for one, I guess.

I want to say that I won't tell anyone about where I've been. I want to tell him I'm sorry for who I have become. I'm sorry his parents got killed just as he had found them again. And I'm sorry we never really had a chance. But instead we sit in silence.

The occasional car light licks the wall opposite, illuminating Cal's face. His eyes are closed. The distance between us is only a few metres but might as well be the size of a continent.

I think about what I've lost and what he has lost. How do you weigh pain and loss? Are we equal now? I lie down and squeeze my eyes shut, wishing the night was over.

A dog barks somewhere outside. An ambulance siren shrieks in the distance, on its way to some other drama.

Neither of us speaks as we wait for morning.

I dream about the stag again.

I can almost feel the crisp Highland air burning clean in my lungs. Its head is bent as it tugs at grass, chewing slowly. I'm full of light and happiness but know I somehow have to get near the stag. But although I keep running, I never get any closer. There's no sound at all but the stag jerks and a gaping, bloody hole opens between its eyes. It seems to fall for ages, never landing on the heather under its hooves, which quickly turns from purple to a deep, sticky red . . .

My face is wet as I crank open sore eyes into a blaze of sunlight. Cal is lying nearer to me now, on his side with one arm bent weirdly over his head like he's fighting something off. He gives a gentle little snore and my insides twist with longing for the days when I could tease him about that stuff. I cough loudly and his body spasms as he comes back to consciousness. For a second he looks like the younger Cal from before and then his expression clears and hardens.

'Is it time to go yet?' I say through dry lips. I reach for the mug of water I was given earlier and down it, even though it is a bit warm and stale now.

He looks at his watch. 'Um, yeah. I reckon so,' he says, getting up. He avoids my eye. Maybe he's embarrassed that he fell asleep when he was meant to be keeping watch on me.

My back and neck ache from a night on the lumpy mattress and I close my eyes and stretch my arms up, then wiggle my head from side to side. When I open my eyes Cal is staring right at me. A fierce blush spreads across his cheeks and he clears his throat and goes to unlock the door. What's that all about then?

'Come on,' he mumbles. I follow him out into the hallway. It's obvious straight away that they've all gone. The only sign anyone was here is a single sock on the landing and an empty drinks bottle lying sideways on the stairs.

We go to the front door and step out into the street. A range of emotions come at me now. Relief at being out of that room. But uneasiness at what happens next. Am I supposed to just go and carry on with what I was doing before? How could I? Especially now that I've learned I really am 'expendable'. I glance around to see if there are any cameras here. I can't see any. If they decide to check up on me, they will think I dossed down in an empty house. And they'd have to know which trains I travelled on yesterday to check the footage there.

The bin men are doing their rounds now, dragging bins out from each house to the roadside. Life goes on, it seems.

One of the men smirks as we pass and I give him a stroppy look. I can't be doing with anyone getting in my face today.

I still haven't worked out how I'm going to explain my overnight absence. A feeling of cold dread worms in my stomach. We walk in silence back the way we came yesterday. The sun is bright but already clouds are clumping and threatening rain. Brown leaves lie in cloggy, wet lumps in the gutters. A woman cycles by with a small child in a seat on the back of her bike. It's easy to forget that some people have nothing to do with CATS or Torch. They have familes, friends. Lives.

We get to the Tube station and Cal stops at the entrance. I wondered whether he would come with me, to see where I was staying and report back, but it seems not.

'Look,' I blurt out, 'I know what you think of me. And I don't blame you one bit. But I promise I won't say anything.'

He stares at me, silently. It's impossible to read his expression.

I feel weirdly embarrassed and shuffle my feet, trying to ignore the heat spreading up my cheeks. 'Well, I just wanted to say that.'

'I know,' he says quietly. 'I know you won't say anything.'

'Oh.' I wasn't expecting him to say that.

'But you understand why they don't trust you any more?'

I hesitate. 'They? What about . . . you?'

He looks at his feet. 'I don't know,' he says, his voice low and quiet. Then he blushes and looks in my eyes. 'But I've been thinking about what you said. It's not so different . . . what they did to you and me, is it?'

'No,' I say quietly. I'm so tired and suddenly don't want to drag this out any longer.

I gulp back some rising tears. 'I'm sorry. Sorry about all of it.' And I turn away and practically run into the Tube station. I hear him call my name as I hurry towards the barriers.

CHAPTER 22

no one's hero

When I get back to the riverside flat, a couple of other CATS' Eyes are there. Jannie and Mariella. Jannie has a cut, swollen eye and Mariella is dabbing it with a sterile wipe. He complains and she keeps good-naturedly telling him off. I don't want to know how he got the black eye, even though he looks at me with that air of a story to tell. I can almost smell the adrenaline coming off him.

I make as little conversation and eye contact as I can get away with before saying I'm not feeling good and heading off to my bedroom. I go to get a glass of water and collide with Mariella, who laughs and apologises. I try to smile back and then slip away.

Curled up on the bed, I stare at the wall and think about what has happened since I was here yesterday morning.

There's a bad taste in my mouth that won't go away, even

233

though I brush my teeth twice. Maybe it's the bitterness inside me, rising up.

It's not fair . . .

Those words keep going round and round in my head.

When I first met Cal, back at Zander's place, I knew he liked me. It was written all over his face. I thought it was funny. Sweet. But then something changed as I got to know him and I started to like him too. A lot. Am I never allowed to have *anyone*? Is this my life, always being alone? I keep thinking I don't care about anyone any more. But again and again, it turns out I'm wrong. Maybe I'm just not built that way and it's all been pretence.

It strikes me now that Cal has been taken from me three times.

Once when he had to leave Zander's, when Zander found out who he was. Then when I thought he had been killed.

And now . . .

It's not fair . . .

I punch the pillow and then push my face into it so I can let out a howl of pain and frustration.

I have to make some decisions. I have a little time. They have no reason to suspect anything is wrong so I think I'm safe here, for now.

I don't think I can do this job any more. Not now I know the truth about the people I work for. But even though I can stay at this fancy flat and take long baths with the finest oils money can buy, it doesn't mean I have the option of walking away any more than I did when I was in the back of that van speeding towards Scotland.

What I need is to disappear . . .

I chew on a fingernail, thinking hard. Is there any way I could do it? My tracker watch has gone. I'll have a job explaining that. Maybe I could slip into the crowds tomorrow at the demonstration and just not come back. But where would I go? I can't use any electronic money because I could be located straight away. I picture the Melters and shudder, knowing I could never try to mask my identity that way. Anyway, they have a genetic file on me, same as all CATS' Eyes. And I have an ID chip, same as everyone else.

But I've heard there are lorries going through the Channel Tunnel that sneak people out, if you have connections and money. I don't know what France is like, but everyone knows that since the Second Revolution, things are better over there than they are here. All I know about France is that they like cheese. And in the South, isn't it as hot as a desert? Better than here.

I sigh shakily and a feeling of despair washes over me. Who am I kidding? I can't get to France. I have neither connections nor money.

They'll throw me in prison if they catch me. But I can't be part of this evilness any more, either.

I throw the pillow across the room and swear savagely. It's hopeless.

I have no options at all any more.

Unless . . .

I turn onto my stomach and clutch the remaining pillow under my chest.

Unless I tell the world what I know. Which is presumably what Torch are building up to once they get their supercomputer built. Hacking into the news or something. But everyone knows they are terrorists, right? They don't have credibility. Not like someone who can tell the world exactly what happens in the government's so-called training camp.

Not like a CATS' Eye. A CATS' Eye could probably get into one of the news vans.

My pulse races as I'm filled with a terrible excitement. I probably won't survive this. They'll shoot me. My stomach gives a lurch of fear and I shiver, hard, drawing my arms around myself.

Dying is one way to make up for what I've done in their name. And anyway, I'm not sure I can live in my own skin any more.

But as quickly as the idea comes, it starts to fade. I'm no one's hero. I'm not brave and good like Cal.

I file a report later, claiming I spent the night at a friend of Laura Woods after a party I'd got myself invited to. I say that it is my opinion she is no security risk.

I report that my tracker watch got lost because they will know anyway. Better that I try to look as though I'm following orders until I can work out what the hell I'm going to do.

I'm coming to the end of my report when the screen, which had been set to receive only – showing an image of a blue sky – suddenly switches to the miserable face of Ray, my supervisor.

A little prickle of unease crawls up my spine. I fix my face into a neutral, blank look. He types something then looks up at me.

'I note that you have had problems with your watch.'

'Yes, that's right,' I say confidently. 'Sorry.'

'A replacement has been couriered over and is waiting for you. Please put it on and wear it at all times. It is an updated model,' he says and meets my eyes. His expression is so blank, he might as well be looking at a brick wall instead of a pin sharp 3D image of my face.

'Yeah, got it,' I say. The image snaps off. I am dismissed.

Transcript of conversation on secure line, Westminster

– Report has been filed now. Baptiste claims she was at a party last night and that the suspect is innocent. She came out with some cock and bull story about losing her tracker. Have just watched CCTV footage that shows her entering Hampstead Heath Station with an unknown male. We thought it may be Callum Conway, who is still on our wanted list. She was seen emerging with the male at Arnos Grove but unfortunately local cameras in that area have been damaged and we have no information about where she spent the night. This morning she arrived back at the station with the male now confirmed by facial recognition as Conway.

– And so?

[Subject clears throat.]

– Er, we were rather too late to get him by the time this information was received. A search of the area has yielded nothing. But we have managed to hack into internet chatter and plant intel about the Freedom Day demonstration tomorrow that should lure a number of London-based Torch suspects to the area.

[Subject pauses, and continues.]

– Two birds with one stone, etc.

– Quite. And are you sure the girl's usefulness is coming to an end?

– Quite sure. There have been reports of her crying behind closed doors. I think her Commitment Training is reaching the end of its period of efficacy.

– Very good. Well, proceed as intended.

CHAPTER 23

expectations
of a peaceful day

I go back into the main living area and, sure enough, a small box with my name on it is sitting on the shiny chrome cabinet near the kitchen. I take the package into the kitchen and slice open the tape. Inside is a Tracker Watch that looks different from my old one. It's a bit bulkier, as though made for a bigger wrist. And even though it's meant to be a new design, it looks weirdly old too. I try to think of a way to avoid putting it on but I can't think of a reason. So, muttering angrily under my breath, I snap it around my wrist. No danger of me slipping away now.

I go back to my room and lie in bed. Memories of Scotland start to come back to me the minute I close my eyes.

It's still unclear and hazy in my mind, but I remember the abseiling accident now. Trying to kill Dan was such a violent action, it seems to have torn something apart in my mind and laid bare what happened before.

Snatches from my time in that Box place come back, like flashes of too-bright photographs where the colours are all wrong. The pain when they shocked me. The horrible images they forced me to watch. And that's not all. Everything's coming back to me in pieces: Reo dying. Christian trying to warn me about Skye. Skye betraying me.

I cry softly into my pillow and finally fall asleep.

In the morning I watch telly in the bath until the water goes cold, feeling a bit numb inside. I don't know what to do next. I stare at the images of people arriving from Leicester Square Tube station, spilling out into the street. They look weirdly happy. The view switches to a reporter on the scene, huddled under a bright yellow umbrella.

'And what is the mood like down there, Christabel?' says a voice from the studio.

'It's very positive, John,' says the reporter. 'The authorities say they are expecting a peaceful day. There are expected to be increased numbers up on last year when a security alert caused events to end earlier than anticipated. But the very attractive incentives package for all attendees has certainly caused numbers to rise this year, as far as I can see. We only hope the weather cooperates a little!'

The anchorman gives a cheesy false laugh and the scene cuts back to the studio.

'And speaking of the weather, let's head on over to Gabby for an update on that rain.'

I switch off the telly and slowly dry myself. My body feels sore and tired, like I've lived too many lives already in my fifteen years.

I think about what the reporter said. I'd heard somewhere that people have been offered credits for food banks and transport hubs if they turn up today. Guess bribery is one way to boost numbers.

I force myself to eat some toast, even though my stomach has shrunk to the size of a clenched fist, then go to the communications room and log in. If I can get something easy to do today, it might give me time to think about what I can do next.

My instructions, it seems, are to help out at the Freedom Day celebrations. I'm to be in the centre of the crowd at eleven a.m. exactly. There's been some intelligence that a protest may begin there. My job is to spot signs of it before it has the chance to develop and call for backup.

Who cares? I think, as I hear my voice say clearly that I understand the job.

The air is filled with a fine, damp mist but there's an excited energy fizzing around too. It makes me feel sadder and more alone than ever.

I walk across Waterloo Bridge and up onto the Strand, then make my way round to Trafalgar Square. When I first came to London I loved to look up at all the old buildings that were squashed up against shiny new ones, all jumbled, like a kid designed it. Now I feel nothing much for it either way.

There are stands selling doughnuts and coffee, or soya dogs and chips. A few stands advertise *Real Hamburgers* but as meat is hard to come by these days, it's anyone's guess what's in there. There was a story a while back about a major supermarket chain selling meat pies that contained cat. And the so-called 'test-tube burgers' everyone went on about a few years ago were so horrible they couldn't shift them.

A busker makes the most of it being the one day he can sing without being arrested for begging. I recognise a song from when I was little. It's being systematically slaughtered now.

The giant 3D screen covering the National Gallery is showing the build-up to a performance of a huge band called Fusion Illusion. I hear that once you could actually see music being played outside like this. It's a crazy thought. I can't really imagine what that would be like. Surely it wouldn't sound as good as an enhanced recording?

Who knows why I'm even thinking about this stuff.

And then the air is knocked out of me as I turn and find myself looking at a familiar face in the crowd.

London is big, but it's not that big. Of course I could run into him again.

Cal.

We stare at each other for a few moments, oblivious to the sea of people passing around us. I feel as though I've been given another chance. I don't believe in fate, but maybe this was meant to be. Maybe we were meant to see each other again. Maybe this time, I'll be able to make him understand that I never wanted any of this to happen.

But what if he feels differently? I hold my breath, waiting to see if he will walk away from me.

He doesn't walk away. He breaks into the biggest, happiest grin and I swear my heart actually grows in my chest. With hope. Something I haven't felt for a very long time.

We start to walk towards each other, slowly at first, and then faster, almost pushing past people.

And then I feel a strong grip on my arm from the side and someone says, 'Hey!'

Irritated, I look to my right, ready to shake off the hand.

And I find myself face to face with the very last person in the world that I ever wanted to see again.

Skye.

I look quickly at Cal, trying to flash a desperate message from my eyes.

Don't come over, I beg him silently. He seems to understand. He stops and quickly gets sucked back into the crowd, which is getting denser by the minute.

With a sickening feeling in my stomach, I turn back to face Skye. She's looking around, weirdly, as though thinking about running but when she faces me with a resigned expression, I see for the first time how terrible she looks. Her blond hair has been cut too short and her eyes have violet marks beneath them like delicate thumb prints. She has lost a ton of weight and her eyes have that dead look I've seen before.

'What are you doing here?' I hiss at her. This girl is pure poison. How many more people have ended up dead since I last saw her? And she was responsible for me being subjected to that brainwashing treatment a second time. Maybe things would have been different if that hadn't happened. Maybe less people would have been hurt.

'Same as you, *silly*,' she says and does a weird, almost affectionate nudge of my arm. 'Keeping track of things. It's good to see you.' Her eyes skitter from my face down my body and back up again.

'Is it?' I say icily. I haven't got time for this crap right now. 'Why?'

She considers me, like she's genuinely working out the answer to this question.

'I really thought we would be friends, you know,' she says. 'In Scotland. But you're not very loyal are you, Kyla? That's your trouble. That was always your trouble. They didn't have lessons for that.'

'*Loyal?*' I don't even know where to begin with this. Like loyalty had anything to do with me not wanting to be friends with someone like her. But I don't get the chance to say anything before she leans in, putting her mouth close to my ear. It's almost like she's going to kiss me but instead she whispers, 'I almost envy you.' I flinch away, smelling sour breath covered up by mint gum. She squeezes her eyes closed for a second and then opens them again. They're glistening now. 'Goodbye, Kyla.'

'What are you talking about?'

But she just smiles and hurries away through the crowd, pushing past people. I look around sharply, wondering what she is running from. I hunt for Cal with my eyes and catch a glimpse of him close to Nelson's Column. The crowd moves like a wave and neither of us is where we were a moment ago. More and more people are coming into the square in time for the band to start and the day to officially begin. He mouths something I can't catch and holds up his hand to say, *Wait there.*

I start moving closer to him, still rattled by Skye. But there is a large family in front of me, with several small children holding balloons and clinging on to their parents' hands, looking terrified and thrilled all at once. This must be the biggest Freedom Day celebration for years. There must be thousands here already. I can't believe they're allowing so many in.

But none of that's important. I need to see Cal. To touch him. To be allowed another chance.

I try not to get swept along by the crowd as a huge cheer goes up. Music blasts out from the big screen and people start to dance and clap.

Panic swells because I can't see Cal at all and then

suddenly he's right there, looking down at me and smiling, smiling so much his eyes are filled with happy light.

We don't speak but just sort of come together at the same time and he holds me tightly. Something sags inside and I know I'm not alone at all. I'm being given that second chance. We kiss for ages and people push past and jostle but we don't care.

When we come up for air I realise he's saying something. But it's so noisy I laugh and put my hand to my ear, mouthing, '*What?*'

He puts his lips to my ear and says loudly, 'But you're not . . . you're not working for them, are you?'

I swallow, wondering how I can explain that I'm only going through the motions.

But that's when I notice something odd.

There were police and unformed CATS crawling all over the place when I got here. Several stood on the lions at the front of the National Gallery with a couple on the base of Nelson's Column, guns slung across their shoulders as they eyed the crowd for signs of any trouble. Others were dotted around the edges of Trafalgar Square. But they seem to have melted away. I can't see a single member of the security forces.

Why are they keeping such a low profile? Especially when they're expecting trouble to kick off this morning.

The cogs of my brain seem to turn far too slowly.

I ask myself: *Is it because something else is going to happen?*

A way of getting rid of me and Cal at the same time . . . plus a whole lot of other innocent bystanders?

Goodbye, Kyla . . .

Those were Skye's last words to me. Why was she here, really? To check up on me?

Cal's speaking but I can't seem to take in what he's saying.

I look at my tracker watch. It's eight minutes to eleven. Is eleven the time a bomb will go off?

It's as I stare down at the bulky thing on my wrist that the sickening understanding seeps into my brain like poison. Some drunken lads with their arms around each other push into me then and the crowd sags and complains. Cal is cut off from me, swallowed up by shifting bodies.

'Oh, God . . . No, no . . .' I whimper and start to shove my way through the crowd, away from the centre, away from Cal, who shouts out behind me.

I know why the Tracker Watch is bulkier than normal.

There is something inside it.

I am a walking bomb.

CHAPTER 24

breaking

I try to undo the clasp with shaking fingers. But it has a plastic weld lock; heat from your skin activates the mechanism to lock it in place. I pull at it, starting to cry hot tears, but it tightly encircles my wrist in its death grip. I think about cutting off my own hand. But how?

I know from my training that a plaster bomb must be completely immersed in water to be deactivated. But what if the wrist band is waterproof?

It's the only thing I can think of so I shove and push my way through people to get away. I want to shout, 'BOMB!' but a mass panic will make it much harder for me to get to the river.

'Let me through!' I scream. 'I've got DRC!'

There's a collective 'Ooh' sound and the crowd begins to part. No one wants to be near a girl with the current superbug, Drug Resistant Cholera, who's threatening to puke. The floods have messed with the water and people have been getting sick.

It's easier to get out of the square now but where can I go?

Please, Cal . . . please stay away. Don't let them win . . .

I finally make it out onto the Strand, which is filled with people making their way up to Trafalgar Square.

I have to get to the river. But I can't swim.

It wasn't something they taught us in Scotland. Now I wish so much that they had. I'm terrified of jumping into the dirty Thames and drowning. But I'm more terrified of blowing to pieces. I expect police and CATS to close on me like a net but nothing happens. And I realise the bomb is both my protector and my potential death. They won't come too close. They know the job will be done, one way or another.

Running down the side of Charing Cross Station I slam into a man holding a paper cup and hot, brown liquid explodes over both of us. He starts swearing at me but I keep running through the Tube station, where more and more people are spilling out.

I can feel the seconds left of my life ticking away inside me as I reach the Embankment, trying to wait for a break in the traffic thundering in front of me. Then I dive out, ignoring the screaming horns.

There are boats lined up all along the Embankment, moored together so closely that I have no chance of getting into the water.

Too many thoughts are crowding into my head at once. Will it hurt or will it be over too fast for me to feel anything? A sob rips from my mouth. How will it feel as water surges into my lungs?

I look down at the deadly thing on my wrist and give a moan of pure terror. Making another death-dash across the road I start to bound up the stairs to Waterloo Bridge.

People are moving in both directions across the bridge and I realise I have to get them away from me now.

'There's a bomb!' I scream. 'Get off the bridge!'

There's a moment where nobody seems to do anything and then as one person understands what I've said, a chain reaction sets in motion. Within seconds screams punctuate the damp air and people start surging in both directions, confused, terrified, violent in their terror. A man punches another in the face and he drops to the ground, where people start to trample over him in their haste to get away. I push on, shoving against the tide.

It's two minutes to eleven.

I run to the gap in the security fence, praying it hasn't been mended yet.

Thank God. The wire gapes open, big enough for me to get through.

But first I start to smash the watch against the metal railings. The bomb must be exposed for the water to work. Pain sears through my wrist and arm as I slam it over and over again. The watch stays in one piece. With a tearing scream of frustration I smash it harder against the surface, over and over, until the breath-snatching pain almost makes me pass out and I know my wrist is broken. The watch is finally breaking. I do it one more time.

Through eyes nearly blinded by tears I see the way the front of the watch hangs crookedly to one side, revealing the pale, deadly square inside. Even now, despite it all, there's a feeling of cold shock that they really did this to me. I pluck at it with fingers that jump and spasm with terror. Can't get it out! It's stuck inside!

I was so stupid to think they didn't know about me and Cal. I bet they've watched me the whole time I was in London. And then I ended up finding him on a job. The one job where I 'lose' my tracker.

Twenty seconds.

Oh God . . . did they know that last job would lead me to Cal? Is that what they wanted from me all along? And I fooled them. But now I'm going to pay with my life.

Gulping with terror, I climb up onto the railing and push myself through the hole. The metal teeth tear my skin and catch in my hair, trapping me. I yelp and pull my head to the side, wrenching out a chunk of hair. Standing on the outer edge of the railing, I stare down at the mucky brown water sloshing and chopping below me. I can't do it. My knees buckle hard and I stumble, grabbing the railing and crying out.

I can't do it . . .

I don't know how many seconds I've got left.

But even if I had a whole day, it would never be enough. I'd need a lifetime to make up for the things I've done. To go back to being the kind of girl Mum would have wanted me to be.

For a crazy second I picture the stag, standing proud in the mist and watching me.

It represented everything that was free once. And it was only when I let that go that I was able to become the hate machine they wanted me to be.

No more. I'd rather be dead.

I have to do it.

So I jump.

CHAPTER 25

river

A wall of icy dirt slams into me. The world goes quiet and everything becomes the colour of nightmares. Vague blurry shapes surge at me in the brown gloom. A shopping trolley. An animal. Blobs of plastic. My arms and legs thrash about as I sink and then start to rise up again. My head emerges. I gulp in air but I swallow water too, which fills me up with its foul, chemical murk.

A wave washes over my head. I'm sinking again. I thrash my feet and feel something slimy catch around my ankle, holding me under the water.

Panic rips through me as I kick and try to free my leg. I don't know what it is but it has me in a death grip.

My lungs are on fire. I know I can't hold this breath in any longer.

This is it . . . this is the moment I die.

I need to let go . . .

I close my eyes, holding on to each second I have before opening my lungs to the treacherous water.

And then something else is pulling at my ankle. In shock, I open my eyes and accidentally inhale. The icy water floods my nose and throat. Darkness starts to close in as pain clamps around my chest, squeezing it tight, tighter . . .

My body slams onto a rough, hard surface. Pain erupts between my shoulder blades, over and over again.

'Kyla! Kyla! Come on!'

The voice comes from far away, like someone is shouting from the end of a long tunnel.

There's another violent impact between my shoulder blades and then my stomach seems to leave my body. Sour liquid streams through my lips and onto the concrete beneath me.

I heave and retch and hear the voice, closer now, breathless sounding, say, 'That's it! Get it all out!'

When I've stopped heaving, I roll onto my back and stare up. My eyes take a moment to focus on the face floating above me and for the third time in a few days, I'm not sure I'm really seeing him.

'Why d'you do that?' says Cal, before having a violent coughing fit and spitting water onto the ground behind where he kneels next to me. 'Why d'you jump in the bloody Thames?'

'Bomb,' I say weakly. It's the biggest effort ever to squeeze that one word out of my mouth. I'm exhausted to my bones and think if I close my eyes, I'll somehow just melt into the ground here and disappear.

'Bomb?' gasps Cal. 'What the hell?'

All I can do is wave my wrist at him, still gripped by the hateful plastic circle. It hurts. Stupid, broken thing.

'Oh my God,' he says, voice cracking. 'You jumped in to deactivate it?'

I nod my head. At least, I try to, but I have the heaviest head anyone has ever had. I can barely move it. I start to close my eyes . . .

'Kyla!' His voice is like a gunshot. I'm being hauled up into a sitting position, suddenly deathly cold and too much awake. 'Stay with me! You swallowed a lot of crap in there. I've got to get you somewhere where people can help.'

I try to speak, but my lips feel stiff and strange. I'm shaking with a cold so intense that my body starts to jerk uncontrollably and I make strange gulping sounds.

'Shh, shh,' Cal soothes and wraps his arms around me. He's wet and cold too but there is some comfort in the strength of his grip.

'There's . . . no . . . time . . . for this,' I gasp through rigid, frozen lips. 'Got to . . . got to get away. They're coming for me.'

'I know,' he says, getting to his feet and holding out a hand. 'But they're not having you this time. I'm not losing you ever again.'

CHAPTER 26

mangoes

I turn over, groaning at the deep ache in my hipbone where it has been pressed against the cold metal floor. My wrist has a plastic cast on it and it's still awkward and stiff after a week, although the pain has gone. My whole body is a mass of pressure points: hips, knees, elbows. I've never wished I was fat before but now I do. Then it wouldn't be like my bones were being rubbed raw.

I've lost count of the hours now.

There's no point in trying to sleep. At least I've stopped thinking I might be sick from the diesel smell that seeps up from the back of the lorry. Other smells are competing now; human sweat and breath. A tangy musk that must be nervousness. My leg spasms and I hear a complaint. I think it is the man with the young son, who is scrunched up on the other side of me. I mumble an apology and shift back onto the painful hip, wishing I could make time speed up. But I'm not sure I really want that either because who knows what will be waiting at the other end?

A small smile comes despite everything as I look at Cal's sleeping face, just in front of mine. He looks so peaceful. Beautiful. Although I'd never have the nerve to say that to him. We're still a bit shy with each other. A lot has happened to both of us. It's going to take time. Hopefully we finally have some.

Central London was in chaos after we found a way, shivering and dripping filthy river water, back onto the Embankment. The panic caused by my bomb announcement led to a few people getting seriously injured, and more arrested, as the afternoon went on. People got crushed and hurt and I feel bad about that, but it could have been much, much worse. And it meant that we were able to slip away without being caught.

Once we finally got to the new safe house, I thought I was going to get thrown out onto the street again. That Dan guy really kicked off. He and Cal got into a massive row that was on the verge of becoming physical when Nathan intervened. Cal told them what I'd done. How I'd been rigged to carry a bomb and risked my life to stop it going off.

Grudgingly, they accepted I was no longer a danger and was now a wanted person too, just like them.

Cal and I both got pumped with the only medicine they had, some sort of herbal stuff that tasted worse than the river, and warned that we might still get really ill. I pretty much slept for forty-eight hours, having all sorts of crazy dreams, and woke up sweaty and sick but definitely alive.

And now we're on our way to France, hidden in a secret container under the main trailer of a lorry, along with five other people. (I have to stop thinking about coffins or I'll freak out.)

We're bound for a place called Nice. I've heard it's hot there.

At first, I couldn't believe Cal wanted to come with me. Thought he was doing it from some sense of duty. We had a bit of a row. Kept saying I could look after myself, thanks very much.

Then he said something I'll never forget.

'I'm tired of fighting. I think it's time I was allowed to have a life.'

A life with me.

I hold the words inside like a present I can open, over and over again.

Letting my eyes droop now, I wonder what it will be like, where we're going. The French hate the UK. What we've heard is that they overlook small numbers of refugees if you're young and aren't going to be a burden on the state.

I don't know what we'll do when we get there.

I picture a beach, with waves licking golden sand that's soft as silk. Maybe we can work in a beachside café together. Live off mangoes we pick from the trees. Never tasted a mango. And I'm not sure if they come from France now I think about it . . .

I splutter a giggle at my own daft thoughts. I know that's just a fantasy. It will probably be hard there. But maybe we will have something we could never have at home.

Freedom.

I reach over and stroke Cal's cheek with a finger. His brown eyes snap open – panicked for a moment, then warm when he sees me. I reach for the last of the water, which turned warm and nasty hours ago in the plastic bottle, and offer it to him.

He leans up on his elbow and takes a swig. I watch the movement of his throat working and get a stupid little thrill. Lots of little things he does get me like that now. I like being allowed to look as much as I want. And even better, to be allowed to touch.

I'm so used to the juddering, swaying movement of the lorry that it takes me a minute to realise we've stopped.

There's a metallic screech as the doors above us are wrenched open. For a second I'm blinded by the light coming in. The heat is like a slap that makes me gasp.

'*Allez, allez!*' says a voice above.

Still blinded, I grope for Cal's hand. We link fingers and squeeze.

This is where it really starts.

ACKNOWLEDGEMENTS

Huge thanks to Brenda Gardner and Melissa Hyder from Piccadilly Press, who have done a great editing job on this book. It's been a pleasure to work with both of you.

My wonderful agent Catherine Pellegrino has been a real support as ever, so thanks to you too, Catherine.

I was also privileged to have input to the novel from one of my favourite writers: Lee Weatherly, whose comments were invaluable in helping to shape the story.

I'd like to thank my friend Alexandra West for her advice about some of the technical detail in the book and also for being so encouraging when she read an earlier draft! It helped me to keep going.

My Daily Bread writing group (Margot Watts, Emma Darwin, Linda Buckley-Archer, Essie Fox and Susannah Cherry) has been a great source of support all the way through the process. And the great thing about mixing with such talented people is that there is a great deal of celebratory cake! (Not to mention reflected glory.)

Luisa Plaja, Emily Gale and Alexandra Fouracres have also been a source of great support and fun.

Working at East Barnet School as their Writer in Residence continues to be be a joy, so thanks to all the staff and the students there for letting me loose in the school.

But finally, and most of all, I'd like to thank all the people who read and enjoyed the first book to feature Kyla and Cal: *Cracks*. Getting messages from you made me very happy indeed. And a special mention must go to all the school librarians around the country who have been so supportive of my books. You guys are the unsung heroes of the publishing industry and do so much to promote reading among young people.

Heartfelt thanks to you all.

Also by Caroline Green

*I'm shaking all over. My brain feels like a computer
whose hard drive is full. I can't take any more weirdness
– I haven't got room in my head. I look around
the kitchen and I know something is different
but I can't put my finger on it.*

Cal's discovering that his life is not as ordinary as he
thought. That's scary. Particularly when it seems he's
the very last to know. He needs to find out the truth
– but, with lies, danger and deceit on all sides,
is there anyone he can trust?

'If you devoured *The Hunger Games* this will hit the spot.'
The Times

'Taut and suspense packed right up to the last page.'
The Financial Times

'A fast-paced thriller in which nothing is as it seems.'
The Independent

*A shiver crawled up my spine. It felt like the loneliest place
in the world. For a second I thought I caught a snatch of
music in the air, but it was just the wind whistling through
cracks in the fairground hoardings.
My instincts screamed, 'Run away, Bel!
Run away and never return!'
But instead my fingers closed around the ticket in my pocket.
ADMIT ONE.*

Bel has never met anyone like Luka. And the day she
follows him into the abandoned fairground, she is totally
unprepared for the turn her life is about to take . . .

Winner of the RoNA Young Adult Award

'Full of tension, mystery and real-life drama,
Dark Ride is not to be missed.'
Chicklish

'An impressive debut . . . almost impossible to put down.'
Goodreads

hold your breath

Tara picked up the tiny silver earring and ran her thumb over the smooth metal. The inside of the locker got darker and then blindingly detailed, like a screen where she could see every pixel. Oh no, not this, she thought.

If something is lost, Tara knows where to find it. But her strange gift has brought nothing but trouble.
So when mean girl Melodie Stone disappears, the last thing Tara wants to do is find her. But the dark images in her head just won't go away . . .

'Taut and chilling. I couldn't put it down.'
LA Weatherly, bestselling author of *Angel*.

'Gets the pulse racing – clever and action-packed. Green's sympathetic protagonists and lucid style make her stand out; at the heart of her stories is a strong feeling for family dynamics and bullying.'
The Times

piccadillypress.co.uk/teen

Go online to discover:

☆ more authors you'll love

☆ competitions

☆ sneak peeks inside books

☆ fun activities and downloads